LOST WITH A LORD

EMILY MURDOCH

To my parents: earliest advocates, long sufferers, and much beloved. And of course, Joshua.

ACKNOWLEDGMENTS

This was the series that I never thought I could publish, so first thanks must go to my amazing Kickstarter supporters! Thank you for your faith in me, and I hope you love this book as much as I do! Thank you to my wonderful editor, Julia Underwood, who has given me unparalleled advice – any mistakes left are completely my own! Thank you to my glorious cover designer, Samantha Holt, a true artist whose patience with me is much appreciated.

Thank you to my ingenious formatter, Falcon Storm, whose willingness to format whenever I drop an unexpected email is fantastic!

And to my family. Thank you.

1

George peered at the piece of paper under the moonlight, and swore under his breath. He had tried to avoid admitting it for almost an hour now, if his pocket watch was still keeping to time, but there was nothing for it now.

He was lost.

Worse than lost. Mystified, he knew where he should be, and he was almost certain this dockyard was the right location – but then, where was she?

"Evening," came a grunt from a passing ship-hand, and George, startled, grabbed at his hat as it fell from his head.

"Good – good evening," he said hastily, but the man was already gone.

Of course he was gone. It was near eight o'clock in the evening, and the London dockyard was no place for a gentleman at the best of times. What had he been thinking? Miss Teresa Metcalfe may be worth looking for in the daylight, but surely this escapade had gone on long enough.

Anyone looking at George would have known he was out of his depth within an instant. Tall with Eton posture, a greatcoat from the best London tailor and a sardonic air that declared good breeding, he was not just a gentleman: he was nobility, and that was not something you could hide, even under a moonlight night in the darkest depths of London.

George pushed his long, dark hair out of his eyes, and pushed his hat firmly back onto his head. The breeze played with a lock that drifted down towards his eyes again, and he drew his greatcoat closer around him. The spring sunshine had disappeared hours ago, and the night was cool.

The moon, once bright, had disappeared behind thick cloud, and the rigging of the ships along the dock rattled ominously. This was no place for anyone to be wandering around at night. Raucous laughter emanated from the nearest ship, and the sound of a bottle breaking rose above the din.

"Interested in a game of cards, sir?" A voice rang out in the darkness, and George turned to see a gaggle of men, most older than himself, huddled around a barrel they were putting to use as a table, with two candles there throwing a flickering and menacing light over them, distorting their faces, elongating noses and ears.

"N-no, thank you," George bowed his head courteously, "but I have an appointment to keep."

"Ah, 'tis one of them, is it?" The man laughed knowingly. "Well, I would not keep any man from his lady's arms, that I wouldn't. You go on, young sir."

The men all sneered, and one took a long drink from a bottle that looked to George unusually large. His stomach twisted, and he backed away.

This was madness. No self-respecting man – let alone the fourth son of the Duke of Northmere – wandered the streets at night looking for a young woman, of loose morals or otherwise, and hoped to get out of the situation with his reputation intact.

Anyone could see him. Anyone could recognise him, a central part of the *ton* as he was, and then he would lose his Almack's vouchers for good. Society as he knew it would be over.

A bark of a laugh broke from his lips. Perhaps that was what he wanted, really. Perhaps this entirely mad escapade was just a way for him to rebel, to get out of society, to do something different.

A trio of giggling women, gowns tight and shoulders bared, passed him as they threw inviting looks at him. George shook his head. Was this really what he had thought it would be?

"Got an hour to spare, sir?" One of the woman was leering at him, and his heart starting to beat faster as he rushed past them.

He must have been mad to take Luke's advice at the club that afternoon. It had all seemed far more of a jest than anything serious, but when George had returned home, the echo of the front door closing after him had rung out through every chamber. It had been too much: he had had to get away, and the last thought ringing in his mind was the woman Teresa.

"You lost, son?"

George started. A woman had approached him, with rouge splattered across her cheeks that had sunk into her wrinkles. She was eyeing him suspiciously.

"Yes," he said honestly, and then hastily, "No! No, thank you ma'am. I am looking for a . . . for a friend of mine, and I seem to have passed her by."

The woman gave him an appraising look. "Young woman, was she sir?"

George flushed, despite himself. His station left him unaccustomed to such blatant mockery, and in all his life he had never endured such a stare. "A woman named Teresa, if you must know. Are you acquainted with her?"

She stared at him, unmoving for a moment, and then held out a hand.

He sighed. "What will it cost me to learn everything you know about Teresa?"

"A guinea," came the quick response.

"A guinea!" George laughed deeply. "My word, this Teresa must be worth her weight in gold if just the mere information of her is worth a guinea!"

If he had been hoping his incredulity would drive down the woman's price, he was wrong.

"'Tis no matter to me," she shrugged, turning away.

George bit his lip. He had come this far, to be sure, and it would be madness to walk away now, so close, it seemed, to his quarry. And what was a guinea, really, in the grand scheme of things? He had plenty of those, and he frequently gave them to people who truly did not deserve them – like his lawyer.

He sighed. "Wait."

As though she had been waiting for this syllable, the woman returned immediately before him. "One guinea, for everything I know about Teresa."

Fumbling for his pocketbook, George drew out a guinea and placed it into the waiting woman's hand.

"There," he said heavily. "Now... what do you know about Teresa?"

The woman blinked at him. "Teresa?"

"Yes," bit back George, his irritation finally getting the better of him. "You said you knew Teresa; you said you could tell me about her."

The woman's face broke out into a grin. "Did I, sir? I do not think I did. All I promised was to tell you all I knew about Teresa, and sadly, that is very lacking. Never heard of her."

George's eyebrows furrowed. "Why, you scheming – I will have you in front of the Bow Street Runners, I will!"

But she was gone, cackling gleefully to herself with a guinea warming in her hand.

How could he have been so stupid – was this night truly the stupidest night of his life? George cursed under his breath once more, and tugged his greatcoat around his shoulders more tightly. He was now a guinea down with little to show for it; nothing, to tell the truth, save for a lesson in wordplay from a commoner.

Was he truly this desperate that he would seek out such a woman as Teresa? Did he have such a hole in his heart, a gap in his soul, that he would happily fill it with anyone who came to mind?

A seagull squawked overhead, and George stared up into the starry sky, misted slightly by the lamps lining the ships, shifting slightly in the tide. He had to face facts. He was lost, with no idea where this Teresa was, or even, and he felt a hot rush of shame at the thought of it, whether Luke was speaking the truth about her in the first place. For all he knew, she was just a figment of Luke's imagination: a practical joke gone awry, unless the papers were already writing up a story about him.

George sunk his head into one of his hands. Where he should be right now was in his study, with a glass of brandy in one hand and a good book in the other. What he was doing here was giving into weakness, that was all. It was not a vice he often indulged, and it stopped here. Now.

George blinked. He had been standing here, irresolute and contemplative, for a long time. Two women, walking back towards the town, threw him a concerned look – though whether it was concern for himself, or concern for their own safety, he could not tell.

It had been idiocy, sheer idiocy that had brought him here to tonight. He heard Luke's words ringing in his ears: *"If you are truly that lonely, George, find yourself a woman."*

As though it were that easy. The last woman he had lost his heart to . . . a tightness, a pain crossed his chest, as though his lungs were being squeezed of all the air inside them. Do not think about her, he told himself. Think of something else – anything else.

The moment passed, and his breathing returned to normal, though the stabbing pains across his heart had not disappeared. He should have known better than to listen to Luke in the first place. What was he thinking, looking for a woman like this Teresa, in a place like this? Had the need welling inside him finally overturned his reason? Had he no shame? Had he no honour?

"This has gone on long enough," he muttered under his breath, thrusting the scrap of paper into his greatcoat pocket. "You fool, George. Go home."

Turning swiftly, George took a hasty step forwards, crashing into someone who fell sideways – towards the ocean, waves crashing against the dock. The figure screamed, and it was a high scream, a scream of panic, and George shot out an arm and held them, dangling over the side, mere inches away from toppling into the fathoms of the deep.

It was a woman. Almost panting with the strain of holding her there, George said, "Young women walking alone should be more careful."

~

"Sorry miss." The grizzled man shook his head. "We ain't going nowhere near, I'm afraid. Try further down. Look for a Captain Briggs, he may be heading your way."

Florence smiled weakly, and nodded. "Thank you, sir. I will try and find him, but if I do not who else should I – "

Exactly who else she should ask, she would never know. The man had already turned away from her, and stomped back across the wooden board onto his ship.

Picking up her luggage, Florence sighed. "*Idiota*," she muttered under her breath. "How difficult would it have been, really, to drop me just across the ocean once you had arrived at the south of France?"

She had not thought it would be so difficult; a dockyard would be full of ships, she had reasoned, and surely one of those would be going to Italy. Any one of them, or maybe several. She would be able to find one with the best price, and then in mere days, she would be back there. Back where she belonged.

"Hie there, missy, are you available for this evening?"

Florence flushed at the lewd comment from the young man, clearly in his cups, who was staggering through the docks – a shortcut many a disreputable man took.

"I pay swell – I mean, well," drawled the man, his waistcoat buttons open and his cravat askew. Florence drew her pelisse around her more closely, and tried to avoid his eye, but there was no getting away from him. "Name your price, missy, I ain't so particular."

A hot flush covered her cheeks, but she said nothing. Drawing attention to herself in a place like this; well, that would be asking for trouble. All she had to do was keep walking.

Her breath caught in her lungs as it met the cool night air, and her cheeks continued to flush minutes after the man's shouts disappeared into the night. To think he took her for – well, a lady of the night! True, few women of genteel birth would be loitering around the dockyard at any time, let alone at this late hour; but then, she was hardly loitering. She was looking.

"Excuse me, sir?" Her voice sounded strange, almost ethereal, even to her own ears. What was it about being out at night, on your own, that seemed to colour everything you saw and heard? Every shadow could be a man about to attack you, every smash of the waves, a step behind her.

"Yes?" came the gruff reply.

Florence tried to smile. She was looking for a favour here; it could do her no harm to be polite about it. "Good evening, sir. I am hoping . . . I am looking for a ship going to Italy. Any part of Italy, really, just somewhere near there where I can find further passage to get home. Is the – " and here she had to look up to see the name emblazoned on the noticeboard " – the Sally Ann going to Italy, perchance?"

The man stared at her, his eyes flickering up and down her as he brushed his hair back, and Florence tried staring back as a long dark strand of her hair escaped in the fluttering wind, and wound itself down to her shoulder. It was not such a strange request, really, she told herself. Plenty of people want to travel the world, and some of them have specific destinations in mind.

Yes, said an uncomfortable voice in her head. But most are men, and most are rich, and most can organise their own travel without having to resort to wandering a dockyard at night, without a chaperone, asking captains their destinations.

"No," said the man flatly.

"Oh, but please, sir," said Florence desperately, reaching the hand not carrying her luggage beseechingly towards him, "do you know of any such ship with a destination of Italy? I am trying to get home, you see, and – ”

The man turned away, and strode back to his ship.

"*Idiota*," murmured Florence under her breath, staring at the place where the man had just been standing. "If you had just given me one more moment to explain . . ."

But none of them had. No one wanted a strange passenger like a lady on her own; the old sea adage that having a woman on board was bad luck seemed particularly strong here, in England.

There was nothing for it. Florence closed her eyes, took in a deep breath, and then opened them again.

There were plenty of other ships that she had not enquired at. It was just a matter of time. Taking her reticule firmly under one arm, she turned determinedly and strode forward, her head down.

And hit something; hit something hard, and solid, and immoveable. Her foot slipped on a sea-foamed cobblestone, and before she knew it she was tipping, toppling over and not towards the dockyard but to the ocean, and she could see the dark frothy waves and they were going to envelope her and –

A strong hand grabbed her wrist, and it burned, but it steadied her.

A deep voice spoke, with a hint of sarcasm. "Young women walking alone should be more careful."

2

_____

George could easily see it was a young woman as her skirts fluttered in the breeze, and he struggled to hold her there, the ground slippery underfoot, the woman twisting in panic as she gasped, her heavy bag weighing her down.

"Save me – oh, *mio Dio*, do not let me fall!"

"I am doing my best," grunted George, using all his might to pull her forwards towards him. Luckily there were mounting steps beside him, and wedging one of his boots beside it, he leaned backwards with all his might.

It was not until he pulled her upwards and she fell into his arms, safely on the dockside, that he realised just how beautiful she was. A warm, frantic body; dark eyes and a clean complexion; and best of all, a countenance of fiery spirit that dazzled him beyond any woman he had ever clapped eyes on.

"My word," he found himself saying as his throat tightened. "I think I will take myself fishing around here more often, if you are the calibre of catch I find."

Dark eyelashes fluttered, and dark eyes looked away from him. "I am no fish, sir, and I have no wish to be caught."

She was twisting, wrenching to get away from him, and George could not help but stare at the way her dark hair flowed around her neck as a few strands escaped their pins. A pair of diamond earrings glinted through the locks.

"Sir, let me go!" She cried, and in shock at her alarm, George released her, and she almost fell backwards, weighted down with her luggage. Now he could see her properly, he would have known she was not English before he heard the slight lilt in her accent. It was musical, almost as though she was singing. French, perhaps?

"I mean no harm," he said, trying to sound reassuring but suddenly aware of their closeness, even now she had taken a step away from him. She was truly exquisite, with a slender neck and a curve across her royal blue gown, just visible underneath her pelisse, that belied an extravagant bosom. A stirring started in his stomach – but it was difficult to concentrate on her form when her mouth was so active.

"No harm – no harm?" The woman was only wearing a thin pelisse, George noticed, and she was shivering in the cold. "You almost threw me into the sea, 'tis little wonder you had to pull me out! *Idiota*."

"Threw you into the sea!" George's mouth fell open at the accusation. "I assure you I did no such thing! A small accident, nothing more; I did not see you when I turned around, and you evidently did not see me – "

"I had not expected you to run yourself into me like that," the woman said angrily, throwing back her head with vehemence.

George laughed. It seemed quite absurd that this woman, beautiful as she was, could throw herself into such a passion because he prevented her from descending into the ocean. "Excuse me, but if it had not been for me, you would have fallen in, to your certain death!"

She scowled, her nose wrinkling and her eyes flashing. "If it had not been for you, I would have never gone anywhere close to the edge – even you can see that, surely!"

It was infuriating, to be sure: George had never met a woman like her. There seemed to be fire rushing through her veins, not blood, and there was something deep inside him revelled in the sparks flying between them.

She was not like any of the women he knew in polite society, that was for sure. So who was she?

"And," she was continuing, "a gentleman would have stepped aside for a lady."

Now George felt heat rising in his chest. Was he to be lectured by this woman? Was she to dictate who and who did not fit into society's expectations? "And a lady would not be out here, in the docks, at this time," he said curtly, far more curtly than he had intended.

The barb rang true. "Just because I am here does not mean I am not . . . and you are here too, *sir,* so evidently you are no gentleman!"

George stood there, his fists clenched at the accusation, but was distracted by the steady rise and fall of the lady's silk gown as she breathed heavily. Her dark skin, eyes, hair, they were intoxicatingly different to anyone he had ever met.

"Your lack of gallantry, combined with your dubious nature, tells me more than I need to know," she said cuttingly, "and if I had known it would have been you to rescue me, I would have rather decided to fall in!"

And with that, she turned around, heaving her luggage with her. George stared at her, his heart beating faster now, anger and another emotion he could not quite place hurtling through his mind.

"Are you seriously suggesting," he said, moving forward to match her pace as she threw him an irritated look, "that you would prefer to be soaking wet and freezing cold, in the Thames, instead of walking here with me?"

"I am not walking with you," she shot to him, staring forwards and trying to increase her pace. George lengthened his stride, and thanks to the extra five inches in height, easily kept apace with her.

An irritated noise escaped her lips, and George grinned. "I think we are walking together."

"I have business to attend to," she snapped. "Business that does not include you."

He grabbed her arm and stopped her in her tracks. Could this be

– could this be the biggest coincidence of his life? After over an hour of wandering up and down this blasted dockyard, could this be . . . "Teresa?"

The woman stared up at him while her fingers plucked at his own, desperate for release, loathing in her eyes now. "Florence. May I go now, *sir*?"

～

*T*he odious man was still staring at her, and Florence's wrist was beginning to burn again – though not entirely due to his roughness. There was something about this man; something that drew her to him, something that made her stomach twist. Something that made his touch burn her skin.

She didn't like it, but a traitorous thrill passed through her heart.

"Where are you going?" he said roughly. "Tell me!"

Florence rolled her eyes. Were all men the same, no matter which country of birth? "Does your lack of gallantry know no bounds? Sir, my business is my own and I am under no obligation to share it with you. Let go of my arm."

"Is this man bothering you, miss?"

She started, and gazed upwards into the eyes of the grizzled captain she had just been conversing with. He was staring at the two of them with a dark look on his face, and Florence suddenly realised just how odd they must look: a gentleman and a lady, near nine o'clock in the evening, with one held tightly by the wrist by the other.

The captain repeated his question. "Is this gentleman bothering you?"

Her captor released her wrist in an instant. "No, just a conversation, sir, nothing more."

Florence stared up at him. If she did not know any better, she would have said a flush was creeping over his cheeks – but surely not.

"I am quite at my leisure, thank you Captain," she said smoothly. "This man and I are just conversing, he is not 'bothering me'."

She could not put her finger on exactly why she lied at that moment – if indeed, it was a lie. There was something about this man, after all, that drew her to him. She could not deny the warmth she felt when she was aware of his gaze upon her, as she did now.

"Well then," said the captain unconvinced. "You just yell out if you need to, miss. I've a daughter your age meself, and I wouldn't want her in the clutches of a rogue."

He stomped away into the darkness, and Florence could not help but smile. "There, you see: I am not the only one to see you for a blaggard. Now, I will take your leave, sir."

But he did not bow his head as a return to her parting curtsey. Instead, his dark eyes drilled into her, and she tried to ignore the potent strength emanating from him. "Florence, you said your name was. Florence . . ?"

For a moment, giving up her name seemed to be revealing a part of herself that felt a little too intimate. And then she blushed at the very idea; her name was just her name. Why did she feel so threatened by this man? So vulnerable?

"Florence . . . Florence Capria," she said slowly. His jawline tightened, and she was suddenly very conscious of his broad shoulders, his serious eyes. "And you are?"

He swallowed, and for a moment he looked closed off, somehow, to the world around them.

"George," he said gruffly. "I – "

"Well, Mr George – "

"Lord George, actually."

Florence stared at him, and felt colour rushing to her cheeks. "L-Lord George?"

If she did not know any better, she would have said he was looking a little bashful too, if that was even possible for a man who clearly, now she had time to look at him properly, was a gentleman of England.

He nodded. "Lord George Northmere. My father is the Duke of Northmere, but as a fourth son, I have the slightest title."

She could not help but laugh. "Oh, it must be so difficult for you, *signore,* with just the slightest title."

Lord George's face broke out into a grin, and she almost gasped at the way it transformed his face. Handsome now barely covered it: a natural masculinity with a magnetism that made you wonder why you weren't already better acquainted with him.

"I find myself lacking in that department, as far as most of the ladies I met are concerned. They are far more interested in my eldest brother, Luke, the Marquess of Dewsbury, who – "

"That is all very interesting," Florence said over him cuttingly, the handle of her luggage digging into her fingers. She was wasting time, she had to keep moving. "I have a ship to find, and you have this Teresa to find, so I think it is best if we just go our separate ways, do not you?"

He stared at her, uncomprehending. "Teresa?"

"Teresa!" Florence clutched her hands together to keep them warm, and winced at the pain in her wrist. "There, I hope you are happy. A bruise will be there in the morning."

"Bruise?"

"*Dio dammi la forza,*" Florence muttered under breath, and then, "Yes, *signore*, a bruise. A bruise on my wrist – the wrist you have tugged up, clenched, and grabbed at almost every moment since I met you, not twenty minutes ago!"

He was silent, and then he did something she could never have expected.

"You have my sincere apologies." His voice was not meek, but it was sincere. "Not for preventing you from falling into the ocean, that was a necessity; but grabbing your arm, it is not the way of a gentleman. I apologise."

Florence stared up at him, and saw nothing but truth in his dark brown eyes. There was something about this man; something different, something within him that made him – she could not find words for it.

"That is . . . thank you, for your apology," she found herself saying. "Good evening."

She turned away, desperate to leave this intoxicating man behind and simultaneously unsure why she was doing so.

"Miss Capria?"

"Yes?" Florence could not help herself; and if she were truly honest with herself, she knew if she had any intention of walking away from this man, she would have done so minutes ago. What was it about this man?

"I . . ." He swallowed, and Florence saw just a hint of nerves behind the courage of his eyes. "I am looking for a Miss Teresa Metcalfe, a resident of these parts who is . . . who is a courtesan. Do you know her?"

A pink flush covered her cheeks and she could not help but raise her hands to her mouth. "A – a courtesan! Sir, what do you take me for, I am no such woman and I deal in no such business!"

He laughed, and shook his head. Could she see a little embarrassment in his rough cheeks? "'Tis self-evident you are no such woman, Miss Capria, or you would have taken me to your bed long ago. No, I just wondered if you knew the area, so you could point me in the right direction."

A courtesan! Well, that would explain it: a gentleman, clearly lost, here after dark, looking for a 'Teresa' . . . Florence was shocked to find herself disappointed.

"To think such a man as you needs to resort to such pleasures," she said quietly.

His brow furrowed. "A man such as I?"

Florence cursed her over-indulgent tongue. "I just meant – well, you know what I – do not make me say it!" The blush across her cheeks must surely be visible, even in this moonlight. "I have business to attend to, a ship to find, I cannot stand about all night talking to you!"

She moved away from him, this man who seemed to be almost possessing her senses. He moved with her, stepping in time. His arm was beside hers, and it was stronger, she could see the strength in it as he walked.

"A ship?"

Florence nodded. "One going to Italy, preferably; I would take the south of France, at a push, but I really have no wish to be dawdling."

They passed a trio of young lads, worse the wear for drink, and she found herself grateful she had passed them with Lord George for company.

"Is that where you are from – Italy?" His voice was soft, more gentle than she could have guessed, given the strength in his grip. But she was not here to make friends, and she was certainly not going to reveal any of her past to this man. She had made that mistake before, and she was not going to do it again.

"All I want to do," she repeated, "is find a ship going to Italy. I have no further business with you, or with anyone else. Wait – does that ship's sign say *Italia*?"

There were shouts ahead of them, and the sound of running behind them. Now the three lads had passed them, and they rushed towards two other young men, and a cry of pain rang out in the night.

"Stop." George – Lord George, she reminded herself – had thrown out an arm, and stopped her in her tracks.

A fight had broken out ahead between the boys, and it was a bloody one. A man's nose had been smashed, by the look of it, and one had a broken bottle in his hand.

"Oh my," Florence gasped, unaware she was speaking aloud. "Not again, no, no . . ."

Unconscious of the danger it left her in, she shut her eyes, but she could still hear Lord George's words uttered into the darkness.

"All we have to do is back away, unnoticed, and then – "

More groans, and the thud of a body falling onto the floor. Florence's breath was ragged now, and she had reached out, as though she had known where it was, to take Lord George's arm.

"This is why I left Italy in the first place," she whispered, and felt the warm comfort of his hand on her back. "I do not wish to see any more blood split – I cannot – "

Wham.

She fell to the floor, eyes snapped open, as one of the young men punched Lord George Northmere straight into the chest.

3

Breath knocked out of him, sky spinning, bile rising in his throat, George spat on the ground and tried to ignore the pain radiating from where the man's fist had collided with his stomach.

"George – no!"

Miss Capria's scream was distracting and George didn't need a distraction: he needed to concentrate on the two large men now before him, fists raised, leering grins on their faces.

"We'll take 'im together," one of them muttered, and the other nodded.

"He looks wealthy," said another one with a leer. "Look at that greatcoat, it's worth at least – "

"We can discuss the numbers later," interrupted the first. "Get him!"

George took a deep breath. It had been a long time since Eton, to be sure, and he wasn't wearing any gloves: but Lord George Northmere was one of the finest boxing champions the school had ever seen, and he wasn't about to go down without a fight.

A sharp pain spasmed his back as someone he had neither seen nor heard shoved him from behind.

"No!" Miss Capria had shouted as George's head whirled. "Lord George – George, we need to – "

Exactly what Miss Capria thought they should do, George never discovered: her voice ended in a scream as the three men – for there were definitely three of them now – descended on George.

Ducking, he spun round to avoid a punch, and narrowly jumped over a leg pushed out with the intention of tripping him over. A short jab with his own fist and one of the men grunted, doubling up in pain but George felt the ricochet in his shoulder which stung from the lunge of the punch.

Another came around, faster now and more sure, but George accepted the punch to his side to get close enough to smash into his ear, disorientating the man who fell to the ground, one hand to his head.

"Lord George!"

Blood was pulsing through his ears and most of his body hurt, but there was something about this determination to survive, this dedication to living that George loved; it was far more interesting than sitting at home all day, waiting for people to call.

"Lord George!"

Miss Capria was shouting but he couldn't listen to her, he had two more men to fell; but there were not two men, there were five. But the thought of Miss Capria rocked his mind, and he caught a slight blow to the shoulder.

"George!"

George spun around to stare at Miss Capria, who was white but staring fixedly at him.

"If we do not go now – there are nigh on twenty of them, and more approaching!"

Absorbed as he had been with his own small corner of the fight, George had not noticed the crowd swell as sailors from each side – how the lines were drawn, he had no idea – had joined their comrades' ranks.

It was no longer a fight. This was a mob.

Time for a decision.

"Come on," George shouted, taking Miss Capria's hand which was warm and soft to the touch, wrenching her forward as he began to run.

Heart pounding, boots thudding, the mob screaming: George tried to force the panic back down his throat as it rose. Where was he going to go? He had no idea where he was, no idea where he was going, and if he did not do something soon, both himself and – and here his stomach lurched – Miss Florence Capria would be in grave danger.

"Where are we going?" Miss Capria's voice rose above the shouting.

Senses overwhelmed, George made out the thumping of her luggage and grabbed it from her, the thudding of their feet, the pounding of his heart, the bile in his throat, the pain in his chest, and his eyes, the weight of the banging luggage that bruised his legs, trying to pay attention to the buildings they were passing on their right; most were warehouses, as far as he could see, useless as a hiding place – but there, what was that? A door, a door open with a light, and what seemed to be a chair and a table?

"Here!" George shouted, stumbling through an open door leading into a small, dingy room with one candlestick glowing in the window – but it was enough.

Miss Capria ran behind him, breathless. "What are we doing here?"

"We can hide here. That rival gang will keep them busy, the fight will soon wear itself out and then we can leave again, when it is safe," George said hurriedly. He slammed the door shut but immediately there was a knocking on the outside.

"Come on, let us in darlin' – we are far more fun than that dandy you've got there!"

George heard Miss Capria moan in terror, and he sprang into action. "We need to barricade ourselves in. What is here, what can we use?"

He turned on the spot, trying to see into the corners of the dark and cobwebbed room, but Miss Capria was faster than he was, desperately searching for something in the room they could use.

"Quick – the door!" She panted, attempting to drag a heavy chest across the room. George started forward and together, they were able to pull and push the wooden chest across the door they had so recently dashed through. Her luggage was dropped on its top.

"Is there a key?"

Miss Capria shook her head. "Not one that I can see, but there is a bolt!"

George pushed it home, and it clunked in a reassuringly safe way. "There. That is the best we can hope for, I think."

They were both panting with the effort, and George's top hat was completely missing, having presumably fallen off in the chase. His stomach hurt with every breath, a tearing sensation that made him wonder exactly what a broken rib felt like.

Florence looked over at him, wrapping her arms around herself, shaking in no small part to the cold and to fear.

"What is in that thing?" George panted.

She stared at him. "*Cosa?*"

"That," he pointed, indicating her luggage.

She blinked, as though he was asking the most ridiculous question in the world. "That is my luggage. It contains all my worldly possessions; why, *signore,* without it I would be totally lost! And what do we do now?"

"Do?" George said with a wry smile. His breath was slowly returning, but the adrenaline pumping through his veins would stay with him for longer. There was a moment of silence: the knocking at the door had ended, and more footsteps were ringing through the street. "There is nothing we can do, save start a fire," nodding at the cold grate, "and wait for the fight to finish."

A smashing noise rang out across the street, and someone whooped and laughed.

"Are we in danger here?" Her voice was quiet, but it was not afraid any more. The fear that been forced out of her, it seemed, and George looked, impressed, at her determined gaze focused on the door.

"Almost certainly," he said quietly, take a few steps over to the grate and pulling wood and coal onto it from the coal scuttle beside it. "But we are definitely safer in here than we would have been out there. This old room looks like quarters for a sailor, if you ask me, so close as we are to the docks."

There was dirt everywhere in this room that they could see now they lit the two other candles in the room, save the mattress which its inhabitant obviously attempted to keep clean. George's nose wrinkled. This was certainly not the night he had hoped for.

Without turning around, he could tell she had taken a step forward, a step towards him: conscious of her presence so much that he could feel where she was standing.

"And when the fighting stops," she said quietly, "it will not take us long to get back to where we were, will it? I have been thorough in my search for a ship to take me to Italy, but I will have to start again if I cannot return to that exact spot."

George did not answer. Pulling his greatcoat off and throwing it onto a chair, he scrabbled in its pockets and found his tinderbox.

"There," he said, sparking a flame onto the kindling, and seeing with satisfaction it had caught. "We will soon have this place warm, and...well, as comfortable as we can be."

Florence took another step forward so she was beside him. Her presence was intoxicating, breathing heavily as they both were, and he found it difficult to concentrate as she repeated, "It will not take us long to get back, yes? You can find the place again, can you not?"

Standing up and brushing the dirt off his knees, he smiled at her, trying to ignore the slightly torn skirt revealing a delicate ankle. "Let's worry about keeping ourselves warm, and safe, shall we?"

"Admit it," Miss Capria said bitterly, disappointment etched across her face. "We are lost, aren't we?"

George bit his lip. It seemed rather churlish to admit he had been completely lost when he had stumbled across her – quite literally. There was nothing to be gained by revealing he had never stepped a foot into the London dockyard before this night, and less than that to reveal he not only had no idea where they were, but had no comprehension of how they were going to find their way back.

"At this moment, all that matters is that we are safe," he said with more certainty in his tones than he felt.

A scoffing sound came from behind him, and he smiled despite himself, still slightly out of breath from all that running. No one was usually this rude to Lord George.

"And you have to find your Teresa."

Her words jolted George's mind back to the initial reason he walked out of his front door in the first place. Teresa: he was here to find her. The intoxicating Miss Florence Capria had completely driven that out of his mind – and who could blame him?

Now he concentrated, he could see the twist of her fingers as she wrapped them around each other, nervously; the curve of her breast as she tried to catch her breath; the softness of the skin across her collarbone . . .

George shifted uncomfortably. This was not the time to get riled up; they were still in danger of the mob that seemed to be growing in size with every passing moment, and Miss Capria was still speaking.

"That is absolutely the last thing I needed," Miss Capria was saying, as he looked out of the cracked window to see if they were still being pursued. "All I wanted was to find a ship that could take me home – "

"Why?" Turning to face her, he saw the incredulous look on her face before she spoke.

"Why? Does anyone ever ask you why you go and visit your family? *Lo stupido*."

The rush of power and the rush of pleasure that the fight had brought him now meant there was far more adrenaline pumping through his veins than he was used to, or George probably would have not replied in the way he did.

"You may not like it, Miss Capria, but we are stuck here, yes a little lost, until that fight blows itself out. So you may as well get used to it, and start being a little more civil."

She stared at him, open mouthed. "Well," she said in a huff, eyebrows raised. "I suppose I shall just make myself at home then!"

The sarcasm was not lost on George. His eyes swept quickly around the room; a large mattress took up one corner, lain on the ground rather than on a bed. There was a table with a ewer and pitcher on, a small chest that probably held clothes, and a chair. There was little else.

But that was not going to deter him from having his fun. He bowed low. "Please do, my lady, and please ring the bell for any assistance you should require."

"Ha!" Florence – Miss Capria, he must not think of her as Florence – laughed. "I cannot quite make you out, Lord George; one moment you are calm, and sensitive, and the other you are flying off the handle!"

"Maybe I am just matching yourself, Miss Capria," said George, barely knowing what he was saying, he was so riled up by this woman. "And the little civility you pay me will, I am sure, be returned in kind! I must say, I am not accustomed to being spoken to in this manner."

A smile curled around her mouth as she sank into the chair upon the greatcoat and gazed up at him. "Really? Well then I am afraid, *signore*, that you will just have to become accustomed."

4

———————

lorence looked up at him, nervously. Lord George Northmere was unlike any man she had ever met; in this small and cramped room, he had . . . a sort of presence. Something that made him appear taller than he already was. She could not ignore the way he made her feel, could not walk away from a man who made her stomach lurch every time their eyes met – even if she could.

There was desire in his eyes, and it was not just for this Teresa who he spoke of. She saw it spark into life whenever she spoke, and she could not help but receive a little thrill at the power she had over him.

"It could all be over in five minutes, or five hours," he was saying, his gaze fixed on the cracked window they could barely see through, almost hidden by holey curtains. "Our only choice is to stay here."

"Here?" Florence gazed around the small, squalid room. Anything to avoid looking at the tall turn of his neck, the strength of his shoulders. "And to think, I had thought that by this time I would be on my ship."

Lord George strode away from the window, and then stopped

short, almost in surprise, when he swiftly reached the other side of the room.

Florence giggled, despite herself. "Unaccustomed to such small chambers, my lord?"

The man scowled, and it just threw his features into an even better light. He started to pace in the cramped room. "I do not like being caged."

"Then that is a pity, for that is precisely what we are," she replied, curling her feet under her legs like a cat, and gazing at him. "And you would have ended up in a place not dissimilar to this if you had discovered your Teresa, you know."

The pacing stopped. "I beg your pardon?"

Raising her arms, Florence gestured around the room with a wrench of her heart. "Oh, *signore*; did you think a courtesan lives in a palace? That she would be covered in jewels and lead you without a word to a feather bed? That her own servants would bring you wine, and then bid you adieu?"

Lord George did not need to reply. She could see the answer in the angry and bashful flush that coated his face, the way the pacing resumed.

"What are you really doing here?"

"I told you, Miss Capria, I came to find Teresa," he snapped. "And why so much judgement? Admittedly, the rules of the *ton* and society in general forbid such ... such activity, but – "

"Do you not have anyone of your own ilk to court?" Florence gazed at him, trying to ignore the very masculine strength of his legs as he twisted on the stop every few paces. "Are there not ladies throwing themselves at your feet?"

His laughter rang out and echoed in the cramped room. "Miss Capria, you have met me on a dark night, at the London docks, with no real understanding of who I am or what I represent. You do not know my past, and you have no comprehension of my present choices. Do not presume to tell me how many ladies should be desperate for my attentions, for I assure you, you are quite mistaken."

Throwing himself on the bed – or more accurately, the mattress on the floor – languidly, he was silent.

Florence stared at him, and for the first time since their rather unorthodox meeting, looked at him – really looked at him. At first, she saw the surface: the dark eyes, the chiselled jawline, the presence that seemed to grow with time.

And then she looked deeper. There were creases of worry around his eyes, and a tension in his shoulders belying genuine anxiety. Though his clothes were elegant, they were ill-cared for. A rip near one sleeve of his greatcoat had not been mended, and the threads had frayed for a while.

"Why a courtesan, though?" For a moment, Florence was unsure who exactly had spoken, and then she realised it was herself. Lord George's gaze had flickered over to her, and she found a blush tinging her cheeks pink. "I mean," she said hastily, "a courtesan. There is no turning back from such a decision. Once the connection has been made, you will never be . . . I mean, your future wife will . . ."

She could not say the words, the heat that had risen to her cheeks now flaming her entire face.

"Say it," came the deep tones from her companion, and she thought there was a hint of sadness there.

Florence swallowed. "Once you make love to a courtesan, you can never take that back: you will always have that connection with her. If . . . if you should ever marry, then that will be a part of yourself – a part of yourself that your wife will never share."

Lord George stared at her, and then smiled as though surprised she had spoken. "I know. Do you think I have not thought of that? But to remain as I am . . ."

His eyes drifted away from her and onto the fire finally starting to throw out heat.

"Remain as you are – remain whole?" Florence could not help but say it as the memories of a man's laughter and a woman's false giggles broke into her mind.

He smiled bitterly. "Though our society may pretend it does not exist, Miss Capria, why should we deny that each of us has – call it desire, a want, a need."

Florence felt her cheeks glow pink, but she did not look away.

"You surprise me," he said with a twist of his head. "I would have thought you would find easy offence at those words."

She shrugged, and untied the top of her pelisse. The room was beginning to grow hot – or was it their topic of conversation? "I am from Italy, *signore*. We have a slightly more classical approach to love-making than the English do."

Lord George sighed, almost as though he was relieved. His shoulders dropped. "Then you understand."

"I certainly do not!" Florence said hastily. "Just because one . . . feels such desires, that does not mean one acts on it!"

And yet she felt the hypocrisy rise through her as she stared at him. He was handsome, there was no doubt about it, and there was a kindness about him that would make him a strong and yet considerate ... oh, what was she thinking!

Lord George's head dipped, and then he said quietly, "Miss Capria, have you ever been lonely?"

This was such a deviation from their conversation that Florence stared at him. "Lonely?"

He nodded, a dark curl of hair falling over his face. "Not alone, not lonely for an afternoon, or a day. I mean truly lonely: to feel alone in a world of strangers. To walk down a street and see no one that cares for you, or you care for. To dwell in a large empty house with room after room of nothing, to enter every house in society and find no friendship there . . ."

His voice trailed away, and Florence felt a tug of compassion on her heart. There was such loss in his words, almost – almost as if . . .

"The only way to feel truly lonely," she said in a whisper, "is if one once had someone there to make life bearable."

Lord George's head snapped up. "What did you say? What do you know of her – where is she?"

"Well, I suppose that answers that question." Florence shivered slightly. "Who was she?"

The light and joy dimmed in his eyes almost immediately, and his gaze swept over to the door of the room.

"It does not matter," he replied dully. "Suffice to say that seeking out a courtesan is simpler than disgracing a lady of the *ton* and being forced into marriage with a woman that I have no wish to know better."

A log shifted in the grate, and the fire crackled. A scream shot out of the dark; it was a woman's. Florence shivered. There were many others out there who had not found shelter as they had.

"And what business is it of yours?" Lord George asked suddenly. "What could you possibly know of such things, Miss Capria?"

"A great deal more than you would think." The words were out of her mouth before she could do a thing about recalling them, and she cursed herself silently for speaking them. If he was paying attention . . .

"What do you mean?" His eyes were wide, and he was looking her up and down now in a new light. "You cannot possibly mean that – "

"No!" She snapped, pulling her pelisse around her a little more tightly. "No, my lord *idiota,* I am no such woman!"

"Then who are you to judge such women?" He asked defiantly.

Florence swallowed. "This is not a conversation that I have in polite society, but . . . well, my . . ."

After all these years, it was still nigh on impossible to say. But then, she had left home, nay, her entire country to get away from this fact. It was no surprise that speaking it aloud to this man, this almost complete stranger, was proving rather difficult.

She swallowed, and she noticed the spark of curiosity that lit in his eyes. "If you must know, my . . . my mother was a courtesan. *Là.* Now you know."

Florence had not been entirely sure what sort of reaction she would receive from this revelation, but it was not the one she was presented with.

"That is fascinating," Lord George spoke slowly and with an appraising eye scanning her once more. "For how long – and where?

Did you know as a child? Did she continue through your childhood? Just how did – "

"You are not in a zoo, my lord, and so I would appreciate it if you did not treat me like an exhibit!"

That temper, the one she always tried to hide, fuelled by her Italian blood and the Mediterranean sunshine of her childhood, flared up to the surface, and Lord George did at least look a little bashful.

"My apologies, Miss Capria, it is just . . . well, one hardly meets the relatives of a courtesan. One almost imagines them existing apart from all society altogether."

Florence laughed, and she could not keep the bitterness out of her voice. "You would hardly be wrong, *signore*. When a woman is a courtesan, there are very few shining lights and pretty things. 'Tis mainly shame, and dishonour, and disgrace. No child of a courtesan would ever recommend the profession."

Lord George was staring at her, inquisitively. "And yet, no loneliness."

She laughed again, and his eyes widened. "Ah, my lord: more loneliness than you have ever known. No member of society will acknowledge you, save for their taunts and their gossip. No man will ever consider you, except as the daughter of his paramour. No woman will befriend you, for fear that one day, you too will be the temptress to bring her husband to ruin."

For a moment, the dingy room before her vanished, and she could hear the laughter of her mother and a deep man's voice, and the scent of incense, and then the cries of –

"It is not a life I would wish on anyone," Florence said to drown out the memories crowding her mind. "And you, my lord, would do well to avoid it. 'Tis not a life that suits anyone."

There was a moment of silence, save for the padding footsteps of several men running in the street, one of them shouting indistinct words that made the others laugh.

"And yet companionship, comfort, even love can be found there." Lord George's words were hesitant, and Florence thought she could hear a shadow of doubt in his words. "Otherwise, why would such a profession exist?"

Florence stared at him; a man with so much to give, and yet seemingly so ready to throw it away. "You cannot buy love," she said finally. "You cannot purchase real intimacy, it is all just a sham. When you fall in love, you would regret the shadow of true passion that you enjoyed with another, for it will not compare to the real thing."

They stared at each other; two lost souls, trapped in a room without recourse for escape until the mob, now passing along their street with torches that flickered through the cracked window, had truly departed.

Lord George coughed, and the moment was broken. "We have only just become acquainted, Miss Capria, and we have enjoyed a rather frank conversation about the necessities of life."

Florence snorted – she knew she should not, but she could not help it. "Necessities? You call intimacy – that sort – I am not sure that I would call it a necessity!"

"Really?"

Lord George was staring at her intently, with far more concentration than he had paid her before. "You do not think human warmth, human companionship, are necessary?"

"Of course they are," she said hurriedly. "But – "

"You do not believe that without them, we are lost?" He had stood up now, and Florence tilted her head to keep eye contact with him. "You do not know that without that connection, we become almost less human?"

Florence's stomach shifted again, but it was not in discomfort. "No – no, that is not what I am saying, I just – "

"Sometimes," and Lord George spoke in a low voice now, so low she had to tilt her head upwards towards him to hear every word. "Sometimes in the depths of loneliness, when it feels as though one is an island than no others can reach, the simplest thing can make the biggest difference."

And now he was kneeling before her, and Florence gasped aloud as he took one of her hands in his own, and it was warm, and rough, and it sent a spark of something she could not describe through her arm and her stomach was warm but it was not quite her stomach and her eyes could not look away from his own.

"Sometimes," Lord George said with a handsome smile, "just the smallest touch is enough to feel more. To feel connection. To feel love."

Florence's breathing was shallow, and her hand was on fire and her head felt thick and she knew she did not want Lord George to let go of her hand. It was intoxicating. It was ridiculous. It was beyond anything she had experienced.

Lord George's smile softened, and in a swift motion he broke the connection, removing his hand and turning away from her. "That is what I would describe as a necessity."

5

A loud scream pierced the night, and both Florence and Lord George jumped.

"What was that?" Florence whispered, her fingers unconsciously twisting in her lap. They had spent almost an hour in silence, but now the mob seemed to be moving closer once more.

To think, she had come to this grey and dreary country to get away from such things.

". . . safe here." Lord George had spoken quietly. "As long as we do not make our presence known, there is every chance we will survive the night."

"Su-survive the night?" Florence rose from her chair, unable to remain still for a moment longer. "*Dio*, I cannot believe this: I came to this dockyard for one simple purpose, and now I am trapped in this godforsaken room with a – "

"I hope I am not about to be offended," Lord George spoke lazily, lounging now on the bed once more.

She tried to keep her wandering eyes away from him, for each and every time they rested on him, her heart seemed to twist uncomfortably.

"When do you think we will be able to leave?"

A dry laugh echoed from behind her as she peered through the cracked window. "What am I, some sort of mystic? I know naught of these types of things, Miss Capria, this is not the sort of company I generally keep!"

Florence bit her lip. She would surely miss another opportunity to get to Italy, and then it would be another day here, in London. In England. In the location of her failure.

"Why are you so frantic to return to Italy, anyway?"

She turned around, skirts swishing, to see Lord George was staring at her with a piercing look.

"You murmured something – something I did not entirely catch, but it seemed pertinent, when the fight broke out." His dark eyes were boring into her, and Florence found, somehow, she did not mind the intrusion.

There was nowhere else to sit, so Florence returned to the solitary chair beside the bed, careful not to trip over the long legs sprawled across the floor.

"Well," she said quietly, trying not to look at him, "I left Italy two years ago. Now I would like to go back."

If she had thought he would be happy with that, she was wrong.

~

"Come now," said George, smiling up at her, and trying to ignore the pull of his loins that were growing ever stronger now he saw the curve of her collarbone, the sparkle in her eye. "There must be a more interesting story than that."

He watched as she caught her breath, saw the struggle across her brow, and marvelled at the delicate beauty of a woman who did not know her own power. Why, if she but leaned over a foot, they could –

"My mother, as you know, is a . . . *cortigiana.*" Her voice seemed to flutter rather than speak, it was so soft. George shifted across a few inches on the bed. "When I turned twenty-one, I decided I no longer want to be a part of such a household. *Mafia,* you understand. Being your own mistress, as a woman, is not highly regarded in Italy. In some areas, it is a little more dangerous."

Florence – Miss Capria, he must consider her Miss Capria – smiled fleetingly. "I do love my mother, *signore,* you must not think that I do not. But I wanted to see more of the world than the streets of our city, and she had no wish to come with me. I had seen enough violence, enough fighting, to last a lifetime. You cannot imagine what it is like to live in a town controlled by the Mafia. I wanted to leave."

George tried not to frown. A mother who would just let her daughter wander the world? "She did not attempt to stop you?"

A bitter laugh, a shake of the head, the glint of the firelight in her eye. "No. No, I think my mother had been waiting a few years for the conversation we had that night, and it came as no surprise to her that I was ready to be beyond her keeping."

"Mothers and daughters," said George quietly. "Fathers and sons. It often happens that way."

A spark of understanding passed between them, and George felt a heady tug below his navel.

"I went to France, at first," Florence had continued, pulling her pelisse from her shoulders and laying it carefully on the back of the chair. "I spent six months there, working as a lady's maid. I was a little coarse for the French – "

"Aren't we all?"

" – but I was not happy. I had heard such stories," and now a smile appeared, and George started at its loveliness. The tired lines, the despondent air: both had completely disappeared, and the Florence Capria now looking at him would not have been out of place at a debutante ball. "Stories of London, of the Regent's London, of writers and poets and gentlemen and dances – oh, you could not imagine my hopes!"

"I think you will find I can," said George, heavily. "Remember, I was born here. I was raised on the same stories you were fed on, and I can tell you from my own experience: it is all true."

Florence smiled sadly, almost with a pitying look. "Perhaps for you, my lord. For the rest of us, it is nothing but hard work, struggle, and despondency. I had been here a twelvemonth when I realised that, despite my mother's harsh words, she had spoken the truth. I was not happy in France, and I was not happy in London."

George stared at her, compassion filling him. "You are a woman who has travelled the world in search of happiness; that is more than many of us do. You are braver than most."

"Braver, perhaps. And *stupido*." Florence rolled her eyes. "The idea that I will be returning home fills me with joy, but the fact is that I will never be able to admit to my mother, the great *cortigiana* of my town, that she was right."

He frowned. "Why not?"

"She died," replied Florence lightly. "Almost a year ago, but the letter only now reached me, it had been waiting for me in Paris, but I did not return. So now I return to the Italy of my family to rebuild my life, without family whatsoever. Though I suppose it removes the burden of admitting I was wrong."

"No child likes to admit that to a parent," agreed George. His feet were mere inches from hers. If he just stretched out . . .

"And no parent will ever admit it to their child," she said quietly. "It is one of the things I will always attempt to do, if I am ever blessed with children."

George's imagination was suddenly overcrowded with images of small, dark haired children; children with his eyes, nattering away in Italian. What was he thinking – was he mad? How was this woman, a woman he had met but two hours ago, having such power over him?

"I am sorry you did not find what you wanted here," he found himself saying.

Florence looked up at him, her eyebrows puckered together slightly as though attempting to understand him. "Thank you," she said finally. "I am not alone, I think, in finding my life to be unlike the one I had wanted."

He shrugged nonchalantly – or as nonchalantly as he was able. "You are perceptive, Miss Capria."

"Call me Florence."

Three words; three short words that seemed to echo in the tiny room for seconds afterwards. George found his mouth had dropped open slightly, and a warm blush and, he was astonished to see, a smile were creeping over her face.

"I beg your pardon?" He said, his voice unusually deep.

She laughed, and it was a genuine laugh now, perhaps the first one he had heard uttered from her lips, and it stirred his loins painfully once more. "It seems ridiculous that I am permitted to call you 'Lord George', and you must call me 'Miss Capria'. My name is Florence: I think it is *bellissima*, and so I see no reason why you should not use it."

George swallowed. You are out of your depth here, he told himself. There is something happening; something you do not understand, something beyond your ken.

But he could not look away from her, and he found himself hoping that whatever it was, it did not stop.

"Florence, then. You are perceptive in seeing that my life is, perhaps, not what I had hoped for." George struggled to keep his mind away from Honoria, and found suddenly that it was no longer a struggle. The pain that had seared his heart was dull. "But then, it is not unusual for people of my rank to go through life just making the motions."

"Making the motions?"

George smiled, and Florence answered his smile. "Pretending."

"Ah." She nodded. "That is not a thing the Italians, we do well."

A moment passed between them: a moment of knowing, of knowledge, of understanding. George's breath caught in his throat as he connected with the most beautiful woman, and he could acknowledge it now, he had ever met. He wanted her. He could no longer deny it, and if she had been willing he would have dragged her off that chair and pulled her down with him into that bed, small as it was, and –

"So who was this woman?"

Her words cut across his thoughts like a knife, and it seared his heart. "Woman?"

She looked at him with wide eyes. "Do not attempt to hide it from me, George. It is quite obvious you were hurt before. Tell me about her."

Though his thoughts had often wandered to Honoria, it felt slightly unnatural to consider her when such a woman as Florence was before him. "Honoria? Why, she was a girl I knew from childhood. A woman I thought I loved, until she decided that she did not consider me in such a regard."

The words held little pain as he said them aloud, like drawing poison from a wound. He shivered slightly. "I heard she married and was widowed, but that was the last I heard of her. I think, deep in my heart, I had hoped . . ."

It felt almost childish now he thought about it.

"That she would return to you?" Florence's words were gentle, and George smiled.

"It was a foolish thought, and it did not happen. And perhaps that was right. I am certainly not the man that loved her five years ago."

She was staring at him as though she was seeing him again for the first time. "And yet, you suffered."

George nodded simply. "And yet I am not alone in that, and I am sure I will suffer again – and experience great joy. Losing one's first love is almost a prerequisite of life, is it not?"

Florence laughed, and his body stiffened at the sound. "I would say so. The poets would have us believe such a notion."

"And yet my life would be a perfect example of how this can extend even beyond the usual pain." George had no idea why he said that; it just seemed to pour out of him, coming from a place in his soul that he rarely travelled in.

She was looking at him curiously now. "Usual pain?"

He smiled bitterly. "Titles are not everything, Florence. My mother died suddenly in a fire, and of my three brothers, only one still speaks to me. A rupture between siblings is a terrible thing, and when you are the innocent party let to suffer the punishment, you start to feel more alone than one could possibly imagine."

"I . . . I am so sorry." And she meant it, too; he could see in Florence's eyes that she felt his pain, understood it somehow. "You do not think it is possible, *nel futuro*, to reconcile with your brothers?"

George considered for a moment. "Tom and Harry are, perhaps, a little older now. They could be a little wiser. They may understand now that no one was to blame for the fire, that it was a terrible accident."

She shifted a little where she sat, and surveyed him thoughtfully. After a full minute, Florence said, "I think they are suffering just as much as you are. Lonely people are often close to other lonely people, that is what I find. You may discover they are just as ready to be a family again."

Delving into his heart's secrets was not something George had expected to do that evening, and it was all the more disconcerting when he was affixed with those large eyes, that voice that seemed to melt his voice whenever he came to speak.

"One day," he managed. "Perhaps." If only he could keep his thoughts on more socially acceptable topics: all he could wonder at now was just what that delicate gown was hiding, and how much resistance it would put up if he attempted to rip it from her shoulders.

Florence smiled wistfully. "Well, I am glad you have survived such a trying time. As for me, the only family that I have ever known was in Italy, and as I am here, I do not think that I will embark on a ship this night," Florence said, and George's wild imaginations were brought to a hasty conclusion. "I am completely lost, anyway, and I do not think I would be able to find my way back in the dark. I will have to wait for morning."

George coughed, trying to remove the thought of Florence arched underneath him in pleasure. "We cannot be that lost; we did not run for long, and I will, of course, accompany you back to the docks when it is safe to do so."

A giggle escaped her, and George unconsciously returned the smile. "What is so amusing?"

Florence smiled joyfully. "You must admit, it is rather ridiculous. I am lost with a Lord!"

His deep laugh joined hers. "It is an unusual circumstance, I will admit – but if I was going to be punched, chased by an angry mob, and barricaded inside a small and dingy room, I would not want to do it with anyone else."

His words surprised him: they had risen, unbidden, and escaped him before he was able to put any censoring thought into them. Completely truthful, they made Florence laugh all the more, her shoulders shaking and her bosom rising in a way that made his stomach lurch again.

"That is remarkably comforting," she said quietly, still smiling. "You are very unlike most men, Lord George."

"George, please."

"George, then." Florence smiled at him. Her blue gown, torn along the skirts and ripped by one shoulder, revealed soft skin glistening in the firelight.

George swallowed. This was not the time to lose his head; Florence had made her opinion perfectly clear.

"It is so strange," said Florence, musingly. "It is almost like we have known each other for quite some time, do not you think? We have discussed topics I never seem to get to with my own acquaintances."

George nodded. "How many friends actually speak like this; for hours at a time? No, it is usually five minutes before a card game, or ten minutes between a dance."

Was her breathing faster, or was it just his wild imagination, trying to take him back to that heady moment.

"I feel as though I have known you for years, George," she said, her tongue tripping over his name. "As though we have shared stories for decades, as though you know all of my most intimate secrets."

"I suppose that, to some extent, you do," he admitted. "No one else knows why I came to the dockyards tonight, and I doubt whether many of your acquaintances here know any details about your mother."

She shivered, and George's heart beat faster. Everything about her was attracting him to her, and she did not even know it. It was to be sweet torture then, staying in this cage of a room with her for hours on end, unable to touch, unable to taste –

"Thank you," said Florence as she shivered once more. "I like you, my lord, though you may find it strange to hear that. You are a good man."

Her eyes flickered down to him as she leaned forwards slightly on the chair. "And a handsome man, I will admit. Though of course, you already know that."

If she had not spoken this way, George surely would not have acted. If those words had not left her lips, those pink and welcoming lips, then surely he would have been able to restrain himself.

But she did speak, and those words of honesty, tinged with desire, were enough to drive him over a cliff face he had known he was dancing too close to the edge.

Gathering up his discarded greatcoat in one hand, George moved forward onto his knees before her.

"You are cold," he said in a low voice, brimming with passion. "Here."

In a swift movement, he swung the greatcoat around her shoulders, and then clasped her hands in his own.

"Thank you," she whispered, her eyes staring deeply into his own.

George hesitated for a moment. Once he stepped over this line, he would know; he would feel her reaction, she would not need to spell it out in words. Either he was welcome, or . . .

"No," she said quietly.

*H*e drew back instantly. "My apologies, Floren – Miss Capria, I did not mean to offend you."

It was difficult to look at her, difficult to concentrate on anything with her so beautiful and his body so ready to possess her, but George forced himself to look up. To his relief, she did not look angry, or fearful.

"You did not offend," were her words. "No, I just . . . I cannot. I know you want more, and I cannot give you what you want."

George smiled at her. "No, I suppose not."

It was only then he realised his knees were starting to hurt. Rising from the floor, he sat again on the bed, and tried to calm his racing heart. What had he been thinking, after all: trying to seduce a woman?

"Do not misunderstand me," Florence said suddenly. A nervous smile was on her face, and there was a delicate flush across her cheeks. "It is not that I do not want to. Although it startles even myself to say this aloud . . . well, I feel the desire too. I am not immune to you, *signore.*"

George knew he should not feel so proud of himself at that

moment, but it was almost impossible not to. Preening like a peacock, he reminded himself silently, is not attractive.

"Desire is," and here he coughed. "You know, I have never discussed this with anyone. Unless you count a very awkward conversation with my father about a decade ago. This sort of thing simply is not discussed."

Florence smiled. "Less so than in Italy, I think."

He laughed, and leaned back against the wall. "I would think so, yes! It is just not a topic one discusses, even if one would like to, and you can go through the majority of your youth without the faintest clue that other people have these same feelings – or similar feelings, I suppose."

"Young ladies do not feel such things!" She said in mock seriousness. "And I do not know how anyone could think such a thing!"

They chuckled together, and then fell into companionable silence.

~

lorence tried not to look at him too closely. My, but he was a handsome man – and there was an inner quality, something that went deeper than the skin. A goodness, a good heart, perhaps, that was even more attractive (if that were possible) than the outer wrapping.

But she had resisted, she had stayed calm. It would have been too easy to completely lose her head, and throw caution to the wind.

Who would not want to? She tried not to glance, again, at his long legs, the strong hands, the broad shoulders.

"I am grateful," she said carefully, "that you stopped when you did. And of course, I am disappointed too."

George's head jerked up, and Florence could not help but smile. "Now then, you know what I am trying to say. I am not made of stone, George, and it is impossible to ignore this – this whatever it is between us."

He swallowed. "We do not have to ignore it."

Florence rolled her eyes. How like a man. "Yes, we do," she said, rather more severely than she had intended. "I want to fight it, at least. I do not want you to think any less of me."

His gaze was on her now, and it burned her as though it were a branding iron. "Or you think any less of yourself," he said, shrewdly.

She shrugged, but his perceptiveness was a little close for comfort. "I think when you *make* love, you should be *in* love. Or at least, what you believe is love."

"And when do you know?" came George's low reply.

Florence smiled wryly. "When you cannot possibly live without them, I suppose. When being close to them is worth a journey of a thousand miles. When not being with them is torture."

The sound of rain started to patter down on the roof, and as the wind changed direction, they heard the terrible cries of the mob. Something sparked outside.

"They have set something on fire now," said George, darkly. "To think that this should happen in England too, of all places. London!"

Florence looked at the light. It flickered slowly through the cracked glass of the window, and it was almost mesmerising in its pattern. Or was it a pattern? If she concentrated hard, maybe she could tell . . .

". . . almost eleven o'clock," said a voice from a long way away. "I suppose we shall – Florence, are you asleep?"

Florence almost slipped off the chair as she awoke with a jerk from her doze. "*Addormentato*? Me? *Senza senso!*"

He laughed gently. "Come now, you cannot lie to me, I see straight through you. Here: sit beside me. At least here on this mattress, you will have less of a distance to fall."

She glanced at him. It was not that she did not trust him: there was barely a man she had met who was more trustworthy than Lord George Northmere. The question was, did she trust herself?

George was watching her think carefully, and he smiled. "You will do yourself an injury if you insist on sitting on that chair – here, let's swap. That way you do not have to feel tempted."

In such a small space, any movement was likely to bring them together, and Florence found herself holding her breath as he passed her. Sinking onto the mattress was a relief, but it was warm: warm from his body, and she blushed at the very thought of it.

"Now then," George was saying, "if you do capitulate to slumber, at least you will find that blanket a little softer than the floor."

"Thank you," she said quietly. "You are a very caring man, George."

For the first time since they had met, she caught a glimpse of him flushing with pleasure. "Few think so, I am sure. It does not cost anything to be caring, and so I try to think of others before myself, when I can. Goodness, that sounds awfully Biblical, does it not?"

They both laughed.

"Perhaps," Florence conceded. "But I think it is an honest sentiment, and so I will allow it."

George smiled, and shook his head. "You are quite beautiful, Florence Capria. Do you know that?"

Now it was her turn to flush with pleasure, and she shivered unconsciously. "Do – do you think so?"

He nodded. "More than any woman I have ever met, and that is not kindness, that is the truth."

Florence could not help but lean forward slightly, and she felt the press of her breasts against her gown, and was glad somehow, hoped somewhere deep inside her he had noticed. Something was rising up within her: something George had awakened when she saw in his eyes that he wanted to kiss her. Something she thought had become dormant, but now was stirring in her as she watched him.

"The most beautiful woman," he said in a low voice.

～

*W*hat was he doing? Had he not tried this path just an hour ago – and had he not been forced back, kindly but firmly? And yet there did not seem to be any choice in his heart, he had no way forward in his thinking but towards her, towards Florence.

"You are very kind," Florence's eyes sparkled as she spoke, "and not a bit handsome."

She laughed at the surprise on his face.

"I am just teasing, *tesoro*, you know yourself how you look. I am sure I am not the first lady who has seen the charm in you and wanted to – to do something."

George's breath quickened. "You surprise me."

Florence smiled, and it was a nervous smile, a smile of someone about to embark on a new adventure. "I must admit, I see more attraction in giving in than fighting temptation."

He must control himself, he must calm down. There was no point in his body stiffening in response to her; this could mean nothing, there was no knowing what she meant. Unless he asked.

"Fighting temptation?" He said, trying to keep his voice level. "What do you mean?"

"Losing myself," she said almost in a whisper, her eyes not leaving his own. "Losing my inhibitions. I-I feel as though I have known you all my life, George. You know me better than anyone in the world. Why not . . . why not know me entirely?"

But of course, he had read the signs wrong before. Was he truly going to make that mistake again; embarrass himself at best, and at worst, offend a woman who he not only respected, but was starting to feel a genuine affection for?

7

---

*I*t took her just one moment to decide. Florence stared at him, stared at the man who she could fall in love with easily, all he had to do was love her, and she wanted him, she wanted him to.

She swallowed. It was now or never. She would never get this chance again, without consequences, without anyone knowing. Time to give in to temptation.

"Perhaps," Florence said softly, a wicked smile tantalisingly creasing her lips, "you could warm me up, Lord George Northmere."

It was enough, and he was lost. He leaned forward, brought her hands to his neck and abandoning them there, moved his own to her face as he brought her lips to his.

The warmth of his lips made Florence cry out, but the cry was consumed by his kiss and she welcomed the strength she found there.

This was madness, this was ridiculous, and yet it was so devastatingly right that there was nothing she could do but tangle her fingers in his dark hair, and let him take full possession of her lips.

"Florence," came his word jerkily as he wrenched himself from her, "Florence, you have to be sure, I do not want you to feel as though I am – I – tell me if you do not – "

She had no response for him; no response in words. She tugged her arms to bring his handsome face back to hers, and the delicious pressure on her lips returned as he caressed her mouth with his own.

The warm stirrings that had threatened to appear all night, from the moment her eyes had beheld him, now rose like a wave inside her. There seemed to be little point in resisting it, and she had no wish to. This man made her feel something no one had ever discovered in her before – something he did not even know was there.

His hand cupped her cheek as he tilted her head, deepening the kiss. Florence welcomed it, welcomed him. Why should she not? This was something natural, something right, and good, and it made her entire body tingle with an energy she did not understand.

As his tongue gently explored the limits of her lips, she parted them, allowing him entrance, and a spark of pleasure jolted through her body as his other hand clasped her waist.

She sighed, and it seemed to provoke a strong reaction in George who rose to his feet, pulling her upwards with him. Now his chest was pressed against hers, and the hand that had been at her waist was clutching her to him, as though she were a life raft in the middle of a stormy ocean.

"Oh, Florence," he murmured as his hands lowered to rest just above her bottom. "Oh my – "

She tried to speak, she tried to respond, but the heat searing from his hands was building in a place she had never explored before, somewhere deep inside her, somewhere between her legs starting to create an ache that she did not know how to satisfy.

His tongue caressed her own, and Florence found her fingers struggling against the buttons of his waistcoat. She did not know what was taking over her, but she wanted to let it – and it wanted this waistcoat off.

A button pinged off the material as she tore at it, impatience driving her wild as his strong hands clasped her buttocks towards him, and she felt something strong, and hard.

"Wait."

The connection was broken. She looked up, frantic eyes searching his to understand why the roar of passion that had been built between them had been paused.

"George," she whispered, her hands at the waistcoat that was half on, half off. She moved slightly, and the feeling of his hands still on her made her squirm, and he groaned aloud.

"Florence, wait," he managed, eyes full of fire as he looked down at her. "I – very much want to – "

"I know." Florence smiled shyly at him. "And so do I."

For a moment, a short second that seemed to prevent breath from being taken, they stared at each other.

"B-but you said before – you said you would not want to lose . . . to give away something," George was murmuring to her, seeking out some understanding in her face. "I do not understand."

She took a deep breath. Was she really going to say this?

"I like you, George. More than anyone I have ever – there is something between us, I can feel it," she said in a rush. "And I do not understand quite what is happening here, but this I do know." Her eyes found his, and there was warmth and desire and longing and trust in them, all mingled with a fear of what she may say next. "I . . . I want you to make love to me."

There. She had spoken the words she never thought she would ever say, but with him: oh, it was no sin, no shame if she gave herself to this man.

"It is like we were made for each other," George breathed, a smile broadening his lips.

Florence did not speak, but pulled gently at the material. The waistcoat moved across the linen shirt, and George, slightly regretfully it seemed, removed his hands from her to allow the waistcoat's release.

The kiss that followed was fervent and deeper than any that preceded it, and Florence moaned at the sensuality it poured into her. Her hips found his, and she could not help but gasp at the hardness she now knew was his physical desire for her, and she revelled in the power she had over him.

His scrabbling fingers found the laced ribbon at the back of her gown as his lips hungrily poured down onto hers. She laughed in the kiss as she tried, eyes closed and almost entirely lost in his passion, to unbutton his shirt.

Before she knew what had happened, his shirt was off and the heat of his skin was upon her, and she glorified in the closeness.

And then the ribbon was unlaced, and her gown fell to the floor.

"Oh, Florence," came the jagged murmur from George as he held her. At first she felt the heat of embarrassment as he gazed upon her, naked save for the chemise that barely covered her rounded breasts.

And then she was clasped against him once more, his hands underneath her buttocks, cupping them to his own loins, and her breasts grazed his chest and she cried out at the lurch of pleasure that ricocheted through her, and George was trying to kiss her while her feverish fingers were unbuttoning his breeches, and something was pulling at her chemise, and –

There they were. There they stood. Completely naked.

Florence could not help it; her eyes widened as she saw the masculinity he had been hiding. Of course, she was Italian; the basics were not unknown to her, how could they be with Rome decorated as it was?

But Lord George Northmere was something else: a true man, a strong man, a man who seemed chiselled out of a higher quality of marble than any of the Parthenon of Italy.

His eyes had not moved from her, and Florence fought the temptation to cover herself with her hands. This was who she was: there was no point in attempting to hide the slight curve of her hips, or the soft breasts that rose and fell heavily with her breathing.

"You – you are so beautiful," George breathed. He seemed unable to say any more, but for Florence, it was enough.

She was not sure how they managed it, their movements tangled in hazy memories of lust and something that could have been love but she did not have time to examine it too quickly. All she knew was that they had been standing, adoring the sight of each other, and now they were lying entangled together on the small bed, limbs heating limbs, hands caressing bodies, and lips kissing any part of each other they could reach.

"Oh George, yes," she moaned as his hand enclosed her breast and grazed her nipple, building the ache in her loins that seemed damp and warm, and desperate for him.

He did not speak, merely groaned like an animal as she twisted, pulling him over her and nestling him between her legs.

Florence stared up at him, this man who had made her lose all her inhibitions and say yes to the greatest pleasure she had ever known, and she had thought to speak, to say this to him, to try and explain how happy she was, and then he pierced her and she arched her back in feverish ecstasy as the rhythm he started to build matched the aching waves of pleasure inside her, and then it overwhelmed her and she cried out in frenzied joy and he was shouting with her, and their climax echoed between them in shudders of mingled love.

All she could hear was their breathing, and their hearts beating in time.

George's head was buried by her neck, and after a minute of just resting, exhilarating in the feeling of each other, he lifted his eyes to look into hers.

"That . . . that was incredible."

Florence beamed at him, her eyelashes lazily fluttering. "I-I never thought it could be that way. That instinctive. That . . ."

Her words trailed away, but they did not seem to need words anymore. Lying there, twisted around each other and revelling in the heat of their bodies, they remained quiet for another ten minutes.

"You may not believe this," said George quietly, tilting his body so he lay beside her. Florence turned to look back at him. "But I had never actually met with Teresa before."

Her eyebrows creased. "That is . . . interesting."

He smiled and shook his head slightly. "No, you do not understand me. I mean I had never met with her. Or anyone like her. This .

. . this was my first time, and I am so pleased I have shared it with you."

Her heart leapt as she stared at him, open mouthed. "You cannot be serious. I had thought – why, you seemed to know exactly what you were doing!"

George chuckled slightly. "Then I have done a far better job than I had thought!"

Florence laughed with him, and he reached out a hand to grasp her own. "George, I am so overjoyed that . . . *mia parola*, it is strange to say I feel honoured?"

"'Tis a very English approach, to be sure," grinned George, his jawline creasing the dark stubble across his cheeks. "Though unpractised as I am in this situation, I am not entirely sure what the recommended conversation afterwards is meant to be."

She stared at him in wonder. She was his first, and he hers. It was as though the stars had aligned perfectly for them, and now her fears about comparison, natural given what he had hinted about another woman, this Honoria – and a twist of something that tasted like jealousy seemed to overcome her tongue.

He was watching her, and he seemed to guess her thoughts as he said, "No, Florence, my darling. This is it. You are the first."

Her treacherous heart hoped he would continue with the words: and the last. But they didn't, and she felt embarrassed to ask whether she would be the one and only one.

"You know," she whispered, conscious of the way her breasts moved as she spoke, leaning on her side. "This is the most perfect moment I have ever known."

Now her heart was beating faster, faster as it was when they had made love, but there was no ache growing between her legs, but hope growing in her heart.

"I could never have known how this would draw us together," he was saying. "I feel closer to you than I do with anyone in England."

Florence giggled, and nudged his nose with hers. "My Lord George, you *are* closer to me than anyone in England!"

He smiled, and smiling, kissed her full on the mouth. She closed her eyes briefly, losing herself once more in his intoxicating kiss. This was love, what else could it be? Every inch of her longed for him, but not just his body but his mind, his laughter, his company.

She had fallen head over heels for the Lord she was lost with.

"I hope," he said quietly, breaking the kiss, "you are not too sore."

She shifted slightly, and felt nothing but a warm, stretched feeling. "No," she replied quietly. "Nothing but joyful tiredness."

George chuckled. "I can completely agree on that score; I think I forget, sometimes, that it is the middle of the night!"

They relapsed into silence, and Florence took the opportunity to rake over his features: those dark eyes, that strong jaw, the broad shoulders that had moved above her, ready to take possession of her – there was no one like him, no one like her lost Lord.

"You are the most beautiful woman I have ever known." He had spoken softly, breathing the words rather than speaking them, and his eyelashes fluttered with heavy tiredness – so he did not see the jolt of love and contentment flash across her face.

Florence took a deep breath. Once this was said, there was no going back. There was no returning from this declaration, and his reaction would completely undo her or confirm a lifetime of happiness. Her eyes dropped to his chin, unable to look into his eyes as she said, "I think the only thing that could prevent me from returning to Italy would be meeting someone I simply could not leave."

For ten whole seconds she held her breath, waiting for a response.

None came.

"George?" She murmured his name as she lifted her gaze to his eyes – and found them closed. "George?"

The frenzied breathing that they had both shared had settled now into a regular rhythm in her, but had descended into sleep in her companion.

Florence smiled indulgently. There would by more than enough time for that conversation in the morning.

8

---

*G*eorge wasn't exactly sure what it was that woke him. It could have been the thin sharp beam of sunlight that found its way through the ragged curtains at the window. It could have been the searing squawks from the seagulls soaring past the door. But most likely, it was the feel of another with him.

Eyes opening slowly, it took a moment for him to recognise his surroundings. A dirty floor – and a chair that was overturned, roughly made and scarcely like anything from his rooms at all.

He was lying on a mattress with a warm and lithe body in his arms, and the sounds of the riot that had forced them there had disappeared.

The body stirred, and a curl of dark hair moved across Florence Capria's face. George smiled to see it, and luxuriated in the feeling of her feet entangled beside his. Who would have thought that he could leave his home looking for a courtesan, and discover a woman closer to a lover than a stranger?

A lover who was waking up.

"Good morning," whispered George gently. He tilted his head back, to better look at her, and marvelled once more at her beauty.

The odds of meeting such a woman anywhere were astronomical: but here, at the London docks?

"Morning?" came the sleepy reply from his companion. "Morn – *mio Dio*, where are we?"

Whether it was panic or just plain confusion, George did not know, but she flailed slightly and leaving his comforting embrace, fell off the mattress onto the floor.

"Ouch!"

George could not help but laugh. Pushing himself up onto his elbows, he surveyed the scene: a beautiful and completely naked woman lying on the floor, looking up at the ceiling in complete confusion.

"We are hidden away in our own private island," he said, his voice deep and his eyes unable to look away from her perfect form. "We are lost, I am afraid to say, and will probably have to search for our way out. We are two lost souls who found refuge together."

Her startled eyes softened as the memories came flooding back. "My Lord George, *Buongiorno*! It is *molto bene* to – *scusa*, Italian always comes more naturally to me this early in the morning. And speaking of which: exactly what time is it?"

For a spilt second, George did not want to tell her. "What care we for the time? It does not matter what the hour is, as long as we are happy."

Rising, Florence picked up his greatcoat and wrapped it around her, removing his pleasure in seeing her, but giving him a new delight in seeing her engulfed in his own garment.

"I am happy," she said honestly, with a frankness that George was still becoming accustomed to. "You are – you are a very great man, George. Last night was . . ."

Her voice trailed away; whether due to sensibilities or *qualcosa*, he did not know. All he knew was that he wanted to repeat the experience, again, and again – for the rest of his life, perhaps.

But this was madness, what was he thinking? He pulled a hand through his hair to try and rid his mind of this ridiculous thought.

Marry Florence Capria? Marry a woman who he met less than twenty-four hours ago? He was mad!

"...do not you think?"

George shook his head as though shaking water from his ears. Concentrate, man.

"I beg your pardon," he said politely. "I am afraid hunger caused my mind to wander." And now that he thought about it, he really was starving. "What did you say?"

Florence smiled, and as one corner of her mouth curled, George found his stomach lurched. "I said, *signore,* that as the riot seems to have dissipated, we should probably – I mean, we cannot stay here, can we?"

He wanted to say yes. He wanted to say, of course we can: we can stay here as long as we like, and we can make love again, and you can tell me all about Italy, and I can tell you about the *ton,* and we can laugh together, and entwine our lives.

"No, no. We cannot stay here." George hated himself for giving in to propriety, but what choice did he have? A gentleman and a lady, sharing a room for the night? Even if they had not indulged in each other's bodies, it would have been scandalous.

The awkwardness felt by both was tempered with the hot memories of just a few hours before. George wanted to watch her dress, wanted to take every moment he could with her, but knew by the upward fluttering of her eyelashes and the slight flush that tinged her cheeks as she gathered up her chemise that Florence would not like it.

And what she liked seemed essential now. His every action revolved around her, his very senses seemed attuned to her and nothing else. When he turned his back to stare at the wall, he heard his greatcoat fall from her shoulders to the floor, and he clenched his fist and almost groaned aloud at the thought of what he could see if he just tilted his head.

The temptation was great, but he was strong, and within five minutes the two lovers had been replaced by Miss Florence Capria and Lord George Northmere.

"It does sound quiet," she said, eyes flickering from one side to the other as she peered through the cracked window, pushing back dingy curtains. "Do you suppose there is any chance the fight could be continuing elsewhere?"

Another chance to keep them there for longer, another temptation: but George was strong. He swallowed, and said, "No, I think the violence has run its course: either they are at home, nursing their wounds, or else the Bow Street Runners have most of them in their cells. Whichever it is, we should be safe."

They dragged the chest from the door after Florence had rescued her luggage from it, and George drew back the bolt. The sound rang out in the silence, and Florence shivered.

"It is hard to believe there is a world outside that door," she whispered. She was incredibly close to him, her shoulder touching his own. "It is as though we built our own world in here, is it not, Lord George?"

Her tongue seemed to caress his name, and George closed his eyes briefly and saw the arched back, the pleasure-drunk eyes, those red lips open and panting his name.

"Yes," he said jerkily, eyes snapped open and attempting to focus on the current Miss Florence Capria who was standing before him. "And yet . . . Miss Capria, would you allow me the honour of escorting you home?"

Was that disappointment he saw in her eyes at the more formal name – or was it excitement at the thought of spending twenty more precious minutes with him? How was it possible that two hearts, two bodies, two souls could be so aligned one moment, and then they could return to being perfect strangers the next?

"That would be lovely," she breathed. "Thank you."

George swallowed once more, and felt a hand slip into his own. With renewed joy, he pushed open the door.

Both of them flinched at the brightness of the sun as it hit their eyes, and Florence raised a hand to shield her eyes from its glare. George blinked, and looked around.

They were standing on the London docks, with three ships before them in a line. Seagulls were indeed floating around their heads, and though it was still early, there were a few men already hard at work on the decks on the ships.

"But – why, that is the very ship I saw last night!" Florence stared at the boat, her brow furrowed in disbelief. "Lord George, I do declare that is the very ship I happened upon, and it is going to Italy!"

It was most unfair, George thought bitterly, that he should be dealt such a blow. To think, they could have hidden anywhere last night, and instead they seemed to have run around in a circle, and now found themselves right in the path of the one vessel in London it seemed to be perfectly calculated to take Florence away from his side.

He squeezed the hand in his own. "D-Do you think so? One ship much looks like any other, if you ask me."

The hand squeezed back, but tugged him forwards. "Nay, I am sure of it! There is one way to find out, of course – come, let us ask the captain – "

There was a pain in his stomach now where joy had just moments before been residing. George stared at the ship, the instrument to remove another woman from his side. Had he not suffered enough? Surely it was his turn to be fortunate!

"Flo-Miss Capria," he said hurriedly. "Why do we not return to my rooms for breakfast – or we could visit my club, I do not think it is far from here – "

But her strength, her determination to discover whether this was the ship in question, was propelling them across the straw strewn street, and before George could even think about finishing his sentence, they were beside the ship.

"Yes, yes; I remember this flag formation," Florence was saying, eyes shining as she beheld the ship. "This must be the same."

"Can I help you miss, sir?" A gruff voice sounded from behind them, and George felt Florence's hand slip from his own as she turned to greet it.

"Good morning, sir," she said prettily as she curtseyed. George watched as she tilted her head with a smile, and felt a twinge of bitterness course through his heart. "We were wondering whether this ship be bound for Italy, as I think it is."

The owner of the gruff voice was just as gruff on the outside; a rough leather jacket covered what appeared to be many layers, and a straggly beard covered the face, which nodded. "Yes ma'am, this one be bound for Italy, leaving this midday."

The joy that spread across Florence's face as the man stumped off onto the ship told George absolutely everything he needed to know.

Evidently that moment between them last night had been more precious to himself than to her. It had meant more to him, fool that he was, and though he had danced with ideas of marriage, she was even now planning her escape from him.

". . . which is the most incredible luck, do not you think?" she was saying, smiling up at him broadly. "And I cannot thank you enough, Lord George, for – for protecting me last night."

That was all she saw you as, George thought to himself as he tried to smile back at her. A protector. Someone to keep her safe for a night. Just like Honoria, all Florence Capria wants to do is to leave you.

~

*A*sk me to stay, Florence begged him silently as she looked up at his stony face. Where was the man she had seen last night – had given herself to, had abandoned all decorum to make love to? All she could see now was a stern gentleman with little laughter in his eyes, and a silent mouth.

"I suppose it is a pity it is leaving today," she said purposefully, smiling at him once more and hoping in her heart he would speak. Stay with me, he would ask. I do not want you to go, he would say. I love you, he would declare.

But Lord George Northmere did not ask, say, or declare anything of the sort, and Florence felt the shame of it deep in her bones. Surely, if he had felt what she had that moment of ecstasy, he could never let her even think of leaving him!

"Yes, what a pity," he said, his voice expressionless and his eyes unwilling to be caught by hers.

Florence could feel the heat of her temper rise within her, but it was coupled with a sadness she had not known before. To think she should lose her innocence with a man who clearly had no wish to see her again.

She swallowed, and tightened her fingers around her luggage. "And once I am on the ship, it will be many months until I return to these shores. Perhaps years."

A response: any response, anything that could tell her he felt a little of the torment that was raging inside her own mind and heart – but no.

"You will enjoy Italy, I am sure," said Lord George Northmere, eyes flickering over the rigging of the ship. "And she is a fine ship, by the look of her. I am sure you will be quite safe."

Quite safe – quite safe! Florence wanted to pull his proud and handsome face towards her and kiss it, kiss the life back into him, kiss him until he softened and returned to the George that she had thought she had glimpsed.

But perhaps that was all it had been: a glimpse, a brief moment when two souls had connected. Not enough to draw any declarations of love or, and here her traitorous heart skipped a beat at the very thought of it: marriage.

"Yes," she found herself saying, "quite safe."

Ask me to stay, Florence begged him silently. She looked at him, really looked at him: the man whom she had given her heart to, whether she had intended to or not. Here was the man to whom she was completely lost, the man who meant more to her now than anything in the world.

She knew, in her heart, that if he asked her at this very moment not to go, she would stay. After all those weeks of worrying and thinking about whether it was right for her to return – after finally deciding Italy was the best place for her, it just took a few hours with Lord George Northmere to change her mind and heart.

He was not like anyone she knew: sensitive yet strong, protective of her and yet impressed with the fire in her. He had not been able to hide that passion from his eyes; how could she have mistaken it?

A seagull swooped over their heads, and Florence shook hers a little. This did not seem real. Could they really be leaving each other, after such a melding of bodies and souls? Why did he not speak? Did he really have no wish to see her again?

Could two hearts be so entwined as their bodies were, and yet within hours, walk away from each other?

9

"I will speak to the captain for you." Lord George spoke suddenly into the silence between them, but still did not meet her eye.

She stared at him. Perhaps it was far easier to watch the glint of the sunlight on the water as it rushed towards the dock, than meet her gaze. "Speak – speak to the captain?"

He did not need to look at her, see the furrow of her brow, to hear the confusion in her voice. She could barely hold back, but waited for him to speak.

"I am sure that after a brief conversation, I will be able to broker an agreement, gentleman to gentleman, to reduce your travel costs."

"Reduce my – my travel costs?" Florence stared at him in confusion. What did he think of her? "My dear man, I am not so poor I cannot afford my own travel: how did you think I was going to pay for it in the first place?"

A breeze blustered through the dockyard, and the shouting of men was deafened for a moment as Florence herself felt deafened by his silence.

"I may not be as rich as you," she said curtly, and this, finally, seemed to draw his gaze towards her, "but I am quite capable of making my own way in the world, *grazie*."

"I did not mean – " Lord George spoke hastily, but then he cut himself off and stared down at her, a flash of an emotion she did not recognise moving across his face. "I just thought it would be helpful, that was all. It is clear you do not have copious funds, and – "

"Copious funds," Florence repeated. "Clear? Sì, quite clear."

They had only been inches apart, close enough to touch, to embrace, but now she took a step backwards and laughed.

Lord George swallowed, and moved towards her but she continued away from him. "Do not take offence, Florence, not when it is not meant."

"Miss Capria to you," she said, and she saw the hurt in his eyes now, a pain deep and yet so far away from her. "Perhaps you are richer than me, *bene*, that does not mean I need your charity."

"I just – I thought you were not leaving." His words were not pleading, nowhere near, but they did contain just a little hint of sadness.

Florence found her heart softening, despite herself. Here, then, was the emotion that had been lacking before. It was still there: that connection they had, that they had experienced so wantonly, that they had relished in just hours before.

She glanced up at him through her dark eyelashes, and saw that heady mixture of strong confidence and self-consciousness. Here was a man, the ideal of the Italian: bold and courageous, with raw emotion threatening to overwhelm at any moment.

"You said last – last night," said Lord George, drawing closer to her, causing that heart, that treacherous heart, to start beating faster again. "You said you would not leave England. I hoped – thought, I suppose, that you would stay."

"Stay?" She breathed.

A pressure on her hand: it was his own, and it was resting on hers in a way that made her spine tingle.

"Stay," he repeated, his dark eyes pouring into hers.

Florence found her breathing was shallow now, and rapid,

completely out of her control. Perhaps it was his presence, perhaps the firm grip of his hand that hours ago had been caressing every part of her, perhaps the overwhelming – and welcome – idea that he was asking her to stay.

But was he? She blinked as she considered that handsome face, and tried to think. Had he asked her directly, or had he just . . . said it?

"Lord George," she said, shakily, "are you asking me to stay here in England?"

She watched him swallow, and her heart slowed once more.

"Staying is certainly an option," he said in a deep voice. "One that I would like you to consider."

Florence dropped her gaze. "So you are not asking me to stay. You are merely pointing out staying here is a choice that I could make. Not that you would . . . would like me to make it."

If only she could see inside past those dark curls, and into Lord George Northmere's mind. He was thinking, and thinking hard, but his thoughts were so rapid he did not even seem to have the power to transfer them to his tongue.

"It really is your choice," he said finally. "Of course I would like it if you stayed, but you must make the decision for yourself."

It was only at that moment, as his words rang in her ears and a few men passed them on their way to their day's labour, that Florence understood what she had been hoping for.

A proposal of marriage was unlike anything she had expected to receive on that blustery Tuesday, but since last night – since she had opened herself to him, lost all thought of consequence and just laid herself bare to desire; then he must have known what she had wanted. To be with him all the days of her life. To be with him all day and under him every night. To be his wife.

The laugh that she forced sounded hollow and harsh, even in Florence's own ears. "I will need a great more security before I give up on returning to my homeland, my lord!"

She removed her hands, and the moment was over.

"Security?" Lord George blinked at her, utterly lost. "What kind of security?"

Mio Dio, marriage was so far from his mind than even when presented with it as an option, he was completely lost!

"It is of no matter," Florence said haughtily, though her throat hurt from trying not to cry. "I will speak to the captain now, and organise my things to be brought here directly. I no longer have any need of your assistance, Lord George Northmere. Good day."

"Good . . . good day?"

She barely caught his words on this breeze as she had taken three steps towards the ship in question – but where she had hoped to hear remorse, or even (dare she even admit it to herself) words of love, she was to be disappointed.

"You are leaving then? You are actually going?"

Florence turned on her heels and stared at him. "What?"

"I just," said Lord George, and his voice cracked with emotion that finally met the surface. "I tried to convince myself I was not the reason why everyone left: my parents, my brothers, Honoria. And yet here you are, leaving me!"

"Going, not going, staying, not staying!" Florence almost exploded with frustration. "What business is it of yours? I asked you for your opinion, you refused to give it, and in that moment, you forfeited any right to demand I act in any particular way!"

She stared at him, and noticed his fists were clenched; perhaps in anger, perhaps in frustration, she could not tell. She did not know Lord George Northmere well enough to discern.

~

*F*ew did. George tried to bottle down the confusion and the desperation to keep her with him, and fought the pathetic desire to beg her to remain with him. Had he not said all he could?

"I am asking you to stay." The words had tumbled out of his mouth before he could stop them, and a sense of relief washed over him as he did so. At least now she knew how she had touched his heart.

But for some reason, there was nothing but bitterness on her face.

"Stay. That is all you can offer me, 'stay'. George, I want . . . surely you can see I want more?"

There was a stain of pink on her cheeks now, and the wind tugged at her hair, drawing a curl across her face that masked her embarrassment.

George stared at her. Could she be asking him to . . . no. "What can you possibly expect of me?" He spluttered. "Marriage? I have known you but one day, what madman does such a thing?"

"It is not so strange," Florence shot back, and George felt a stirring within him, a flutter of hope, of confusion, of desperate longing and acceptance that he can never have her – a medley of pain and pleasure he could not decipher. "But evidently, no. You do not wish it."

Now was the moment, George knew, to speak up. To say that throwing caution to the wind and ignoring convention, of finding his hope and happiness in her forever would be his delight, that he loved her.

Loved her. Did he love her? Was this raging passion love, or was it just lust? How could he tell? Could he really commit himself, forever, to a woman he had met less than a day ago, on a hunch?

The flicker of joy in Florence Capria's eyes died. "I see."

Panic flooded his lungs. "No – no, you do not!"

"'Tis of no matter," she said dully. "I cannot change my plans simply because I got lost with you, and neither can you, I see that."

George didn't have the words. "No, no I do not mean – but I also do not mean – Florence, wait!"

The woman that sparked such intense emotions in him was walking away, and in a desperate moment of panic, his hand shot to his pocketbook.

If he could not be with her, at least he could provide for her.

"Here; here take it." One inelegant movement tried to place a ten pound note into her reticule, but she shook him off.

"Have I not told you before? I do not want your charity."

Exasperated, he tossed his head. "You know full well I do not intend it as charity, it is more a – a sign of my goodwill, I suppose, from friendship. From gratitude, for last night. . ."

At first, Florence did not entirely catch his meaning. She stood there silently, her hair unpinned and freely flowing down her back like a waterfall, the cold breeze chilling her hands as the realisation of what he meant chilled her heart.

"Your pity and your misplaced *gratitude* for what happened last night," she spat, that Italian temper that she saw no reason to hide now rising up through her throat leaving a bitter taste and overcoming her tongue, "are not wanted, *my Lord.*"

She turned, barely able to see, completely unable to think, just able to feel. The ship seemed to sway before her, or was that her own luggage moving side to side? Was he really trying to –

"Florence!"

But she was on the gangplank now, and she was moving quickly, and the captain's hands were reaching out and in a split second she was aboard, ready to disappear, ready to leave this wretched island, once and for all.

"I suppose I should know better!" His words rang out into the morning air, and Florence winced to hear the bitterness and hurt in his tones. "No woman of good reputation would ever get lost with me; you must be a courtesan after all! Here, Miss Florence: your earnings."

And then banknotes, fluttering and cascading in the air, great shrieks and shouts from others walking up the dockyards, and the ship moved, and as Florence was taken away down the Thames she did not look away from the tall man with the strong shoulders and tormented eyes.

10

*T*he door slammed shut.

"Why the long face, you rascal?"

George's head snapped up, but it drooped down again when he saw who it was.

"What are you doing here?" He asked bad-temperedly. "I thought you would be too busy at Lady Johnston's ball?"

His elder brother strode across the library and threw himself gracefully into an armchair, his legs dangling over one of the sides. "Well, I had had my fill of dancing by the time young Rebecca came along, and when I discovered she was engaged to dance with young Simon for the rest of the evening, I gave it up as a lost cause."

George stared at the fire in the grate instead of his brother. When he had told his housekeeper he had wanted to be alone, she had insisted on bringing him a large brandy – and now, it seems, she was perfectly happy to let his brother through to disturb him.

"I want to be alone," he said, the phrase dull on his tongue, he had repeated it so often that day. "Apologies, Luke, but I am simply not up to company this evening."

He did not need to look up to see the smirk. "Teresa turn you down, then?"

"What?"

His brother laughed at the swift reaction, and George scowled at him. "Why are you here, really, Luke?"

The Marquis of Dewsbury shrugged. "When I recommend a dearest family member visit a courtesan, dear boy, do you think I am going to let the matter rest there? Oh no, it is my duty to see how the visit went!"

"You just want the gory details," George muttered, turning his head back to the fire and loosening his cravat from his neck.

Luke grinned. "You bet I do."

George rolled his eyes. It had been exactly this way when they were children: George desperate for solitude in a house thronging with people at all times, and Luke had relished teasing his little brother.

"I have no wish to talk about it," he muttered as a log fell in the grate. "Please, Luke. I . . . I am not feeling well."

Luke stood up lazily, and looked around the room for the brandy. Finding nothing but a whisky decanter, he strode over and started to help himself. "Now then, that sounds a little like lovesickness, if you ask me."

George did not answer. All he could hear was Florence's words ringing in his head: *I cannot change my plans simply because I got lost with you, and neither can you, I see that.*

What had he done – had he thrown away the best chance of happiness he was ever to see, and just for the sake of propriety?

"Your silence suggests I am right."

George shook his head as Luke made his way back to his armchair, but as he sat down, he affixed his younger brother with a rather more serious look.

"You did not fall for Teresa, did you? You have to understand, George, you are just one of many for her, and you cannot – "

"It is not her," George intercut.

Luke stared at him for a moment. "Then – by God, then who?"

The flames seemed like a much safer place to look, but each tongue of fire that crept up the grate reminded George of the locks of hair that flowed freely across the mattress when he had laid Florence down, completely naked, ready for him, welcoming him in.

It was too much. He turned away, and saw his brother had a look of genuine concern on his face.

"George, you know you can confide in me," Luke said quietly. "I know I jest worse than the Regent himself, but we are brothers."

George snorted. "Not that that has meant much to some people."

His brother rolled his eyes. "Enough. It is time you, Tom, and Harry started to have a conversation about that, but this is not the time. Tell me about her."

There was no way to prevent it. George smiled as he remembered that ridiculous meeting, of her tottering over the edge, almost falling into the Thames – of the mob that grew after their fight, of the flight around the docks, and finally, getting hopelessly lost and finding shelter in the smallest of rooms, that would soon hold the greatest of joys.

"Her name," he said eventually, "is Florence. I met her at the dockyard, whilst looking for Teresa – who, by the way, is almost impossible to find."

"It does not appear to have prevented you from an interesting evening," remarked Luke.

George smiled, and finally the happiness and pain that Florence had sparked in him leaked out. "You know, I think it was the most interesting night of my life. Florence is Italian, you see – fiery temper, do not cross her, take it from me – and we had to take refuge in a . . . well, I think you would call it a hovel."

"A hovel?"

"It was more of a servant's room, but it was dank, and small, and yet fit for purpose. All we wanted to do was hide whilst the mob ran out of energy outside."

Luke stared at his brother as though he had never seen him before. "Good God man, that sounds terrible! Did the Bow Street Runners come and swiftly disperse them?"

George shook his head. "No, we were there all night."

"This is the most perfect moment I have ever known. I could never have

known how this would draw us together. I feel closer to you than I do with anyone in England."

Luke smiled broadly. "I would never have thought it of you, George; you seduced her, did you not?"

It seemed ridiculous to attempt to lie, so he replied, "Yes."

His glass of brandy was beside him on a small table, and he drew it to his lips. Perhaps the fire in his throat would distract him from the pain in his chest at the thought of that incredible night.

"My word, but that is – George, I am impressed!" And Luke looked it. Eyes wide open, smile still there, he stared at his brother in amazement. "I never thought you would be the one to tup a girl in an alley!"

"It was not like that!" George said sharply. "Florence is no girl you pick up off the street, she is practically a lady in Italy – and it was not an alley. Florence is – speaking with her was like no one else I have ever . . . do not speak of her like that."

Silence fell between them for almost a minute as the two men stared at each other; one angry and hurting, the other merely intrigued.

And then Luke's smile faltered. "Oh, George. You fell in love with her."

"Is it any wonder?" George said stiffly. "I tell you, England does not hold the like. She is everything I could ever – witty, passionate, beautiful, Luke, so beautiful that at times it hurt to look at her. And when we made love . . ."

His voice trailed off as his eyes were dragged, unconsciously, back to the fire. It was almost like looking at her, that untamed fire.

"So when will I meet her?" Luke asked jovially. "Before the wedding, I hope."

A sharp pain stabbed through George's heart again, and he sighed. "You will not be meeting her."

"Oh, now come on, George, I promise I will keep my hands to myself!" Luke's protestations fell silent as he watched his brother's face. "There is not going to be a wedding, is there? God's teeth, George, what did you do?"

"What did I – what did *I* do?"

"You cannot tell me you did not offer marriage."

George flushed. "It was not – it was a great deal more complicated than that, Luke!"

His brother swore quietly under his breath. "George, you meet a woman who you say is your ideal match, you spend a supposedly heady evening of lovemaking and conversation, and then you abandon her at the docks the next morning and come home to be morose?"

"I told you, 'tis complicated," George returned, glancing at his brother as he said, "At this very moment, she is on a ship to Italy."

Luke sighed and shook his head. "I would have thought you could stop her, if you had wanted to."

George flinched at the memory of his own words. *"Of course I would like it if you stayed, but you must make the decision for yourself."*

"No, I do not think so," George said firmly, and the lie bit into his soul. "She was determined to go."

Luke took a large gulp of whisky, and then affixed his eyes on his brother. "George Northmere, you absolute fool. Any woman willing to open herself up like that – emotionally, yes, as well as with her body – is worth keeping. Worth *pursuing*. You know where she is, and you know where she is going. What the devil are you doing here?"

～

Florence's lungs were filled with salty air, but the headache that had dogged her all day persisted, and she raised a heavy hand to it as she looked out across the sea on the deck.

Surely it would disappear soon; perhaps when they were in open waters. She had not realised just long the Thames was, how much time it would take for them to reach the ocean. Even now, they were still hugging the coastline of this wretched country.

"Where are we?" She asked a passing shipman, who bowed his head before he answered.

"Just outside Dover, my lady, picking up some supplies before we head out to sea."

He did not stay long enough for her to question him further, but his words were sufficient. Dover for supplies, and then Italy bound: as far away from Lord George Northmere as it was possible for her to be.

The thought of him wrenched her stomach, and she drew her pelisse around her more tightly. Try as she might, it seemed absolutely impossible to ignore the frequent thoughts that led her back to him.

Perhaps if he had been less handsome. Perhaps if he had been more sure of himself; a brute, rather than a man with great sensitivities, obvious compassion, and a clear desire for her.

For every part of her.

Florence shook her head. This was madness, madness! He had said one true thing in that terrible argument on the dock: they had only met days before, and who decides to marry a person they had only just met?

An image of herself in her favourite blue gown at the church steps with George, beaming at her, standing in a high waisted jacket and top hat, flashed through her mind.

Her traitorous heart leapt. No, that was beyond unlikely. Had she not essentially asked *him* to marry *her*? A shameful thing – and if she was honest with herself, far more like her mother than she would care to admit.

"You feeling well, my lady?"

The gruff voice of the captain sounded behind her, and Florence turned to smile wanly at him. "Quite well, thank you. A little headache perhaps, nothing more."

He grunted, and joined her in leaning at the handrail of the deck. " 'Tis a beautiful sight, Dover. I am not surprised you wanted to see it; last look at home, that is."

"Your home, *signore*," Florence said with a smile. "My home is before us."

The captain nodded. "Aye, I remember now. 'Tis a shame you

cannot find a home here, in England; best place in the world, if you ask me, and I have seen rather a lot of it in my time."

Florence smiled. The patriotism of Englishmen was indeed to be found the world over. "I have not found much joy in England, sadly."

The arching of her back, the slow but steady movement of his hands, the tingle of his fingers as they caressed her body –

"Now that is a real shame," came the captain's voice, breaking into her memories.

"Yes," said Florence, hardly listening now. The memories of George's words were echoing in her mind still, but now she came to think of it, they were more full of love than she had noticed at the time.

"I am asking you to stay."

The way he looked at her: hungrily, and not just for her skin but for her mind. Those conversations, baring themselves to each other, far more naked and vulnerable than when he had gently taken her into his arms and made love to her.

"You are the most beautiful woman I have ever known."

And if she was honest with herself, Florence knew the emotions stirring in her own breast were not just pain, and hurt, but care, and devotion, and . . . love.

She loved him. She loved the deep emotion he felt, she loved the wit that sparkled when he felt sure of himself, and she loved the awkwardness he descended into when he felt wrong-footed. She loved Lord George Northmere – she loved him, and she was standing on a ship about to take her hundreds of miles away from him!

"Captain," Florence said quickly, turning to her companion. "I – I have to stay. I need to stay here, in England. I do not want to go to Italy anymore."

And that was the truth. Her joy was all in England, and what did she have in Italy: memories, painful ones at that, and family stories. She could not live with stories, and stories would not make her happy.

Nothing and no one could make her as happy as George.

"Ah, 'tis like that, is it?" The captain smiled at her. "I must warn you, my lady, this is the last ship going to Italy I know of for many months. If you disembark now, it will be many moons afore you have the chance again to – "

"I will take that chance," Florence said firmly. "I was completely lost when I boarded this ship, but now . . . now I know exactly where I need to be."

There must have been something in her gaze that convinced him, because the captain nodded slowly and barked out an order immediately acted upon.

"'Tis a long way back to London," the captain said hoarsely as he stood with her on the Dover dock, handing over her luggage. "Are you quite sure you know the way?"

Florence beamed. "Not the faintest idea, I am afraid, but I am sure someone will be able to point me in the right direction. I cannot be lost, really. I will find him."

11

A scream pierced George's brandy-soaked head, and he groaned.

"What – what the . . ?"

He was lying face down on the sheets of his bed, fully dressed, and at an angle. He had evidently not made it to bed, and had either been carried and deposited there by his brother Luke, or his butler Morgan; and he could not think which was more embarrassing.

A torrent of angry words was being hurriedly shouted from what sounded like the bottom of the stairs, and George lifted his head slightly.

The curtains were not illuminated by daylight. It could not be morning yet?

A crash, the sound of breaking china. What in God's name were they doing downstairs?

George rolled over and stared at the ceiling. Even now, head heavy from a night filled with more brandy than sleep, and with some sort of calamitous noise occurring in the hallway, all he could think about was Florence Capria.

She had completely enslaved his heart, and he was lost to it – was happily lost to it. If only he had not lost her also, there would be nothing on his mind whatsoever.

"No, Lord George is not to be disturbed!"

That voice was male, and slightly irritated. George closed his eyes and smiled gently. Morgan was such an eminent butler, it was always such a comfort to have him guarding the gates.

"Madam!"

The last cry was accompanied with another crash and glass-like tinkling as something that sounded to George's ear very expensive had a swift introduction to the floor.

He sighed and opened his eyes. There was nothing for it. whatever it was, whoever it was, they were not going to go without seeing him. Well, they could see him for all of the ten seconds it took him to dismiss them, and then he could crawl back into bed, and properly this time.

Despite his best efforts, it took George two tries to sit up. There was a large glass of liquid beside his bed that looked disgusting, but was Morgan's secret hangover cure, and after resolutely holding the glass under his nose for a full minute (during which another loud bang told him a door downstairs had been slammed), he swallowed it.

Coughing, and with a head now clear because it had been emptied of all his brains, George shook himself. Time to remove this rapscallion, and get back to bed.

"My Lord George, I apologise for the disturbance."

That was a sign of a good butler, I suppose, George thought with a rue smile as he rose to his feet. One simply did not hear them enter a room.

"It is quite alright, Morgan. What in heaven's name is going on down there?"

"A small issue of an intruder, Lord George, but it is of no matter, the parlour maids and I – "

"Not a gentleman with more bills of my father's?"

His butler coloured slightly, as he always did at the mention of money, but shook his head. "No, sir, 'tis a young lady. She is talking on so about Italy and a ship and not being lost; clearly not quite right in her mind, but she is harmless."

George stopped tying his cravat instantly and let it fall to his chest. "Italy . . . ship . . . lost?"

Morgan nodded. "As I say, sir, we will soon have her moved along, and – "

"It is Florence," whispered George. He was not speaking to Morgan, not really, just himself. Could it be true; was it merely wishful thinking that heard her fiery anger in the uproar downstairs? Though it was her style, of course, any excuse for her temper to rise.

His butler was looking at his master, bewildered. "Florence, sir? The baker's daughter, who brings around the bread on a Thursday?"

George burst into laughter. "Old MacIntosh's daughter? My word, Morgan, no, would that not be a turnup for the books! No, Miss Florence Capria is a – well, an acquaintance, I suppose you would call her."

To think she could be here – here, in this very house. In his house! Here, when he had thought her miles away by now, on her way to Italy to build a new life.

So what was he doing, standing here?

Rushing past Morgan who cried, "My Lord George!" who was roundly ignored, George threw open the door and reached the top of the staircase in seconds. There was a woman down there; a woman with long dark hair, unkempt and tangled, with a few leaves caught at the ends.

She was arguing fiercely with his cook.

" – and I do not care, *non importante*, it is so early!" She was saying, throwing her head back and glaring imperiously at the woman before her. "Lord George will see me, I say, all you have to do is – "

"Tell him you are here." George said quietly, but his deep voice cut across the space between them and Florence Capria broke off, and stared around her, looking for the source of the sound.

Her eyes widened when she saw him. "George!"

"Florence Capria, I must apologise." George spoke quietly as he ran down the stairs, stopping just before the woman he loved and hushing away his cook who scampered back off to her kitchen. "Florence, what I fool I was! There you were, before me in all your glory, and I was too cowardly – too proud to do anything about it!"

For a moment, he thought he saw the flash of anger that he was beginning to know so well alight in her eyes again; but then they softened, and she smiled.

"Ah, *amore*, I hardly gave you a choice, did I? There you were, pouring your heart out to me about how lonely you were, and what did I do the very next morning?"

George swallowed, so painful was the memory. "You . . . you left me."

A sparkling tear did fall from Florence's eyes as she gazed up at him. "I did. It was the *più stupido* thing I have ever done; always I am on the move, always searching for something to fulfil me. And when I found it, I left it, like the fool I was."

~

$\mathcal{F}$lorence could feel the stress and panic that had been her sole companion all those hours in that dark night slipping away from her, the balm of George's presence enough to restore her.

"Thank you," he was saying, "for coming to find me. For being so brave to be the one to come back, I should have gone after you, but I was so afraid I – I was not wanted."

She smiled at him, and shook her head. "Yours was the face I wanted to see, the moment that you fell beyond my sight at the dockyard. Before I reached Dover, my heart knew I had made a mistake, and when I discovered there was no turning back if I continued on, I just had to disembark, I had to find you!"

Florence had been worried then; anxious she was making a wrong decision. She was not anxious now; every nerve in her body told her she was exactly where she should be.

"But how did you?" George was asking, a wondering smile

creasing his cheeks. "Florence, there is a whole country here and it took you just one night to find me?"

"You forget," she said coyly, "a very rude man threw a great deal of money at me recently. The captain had gathered it up, and decided that it belonged to me as I left him."

He laughed, and shook his head wryly. "I have certainly met my match in you!"

Florence beamed at him. "It turns out money can not only speed up horses, but also loosen tongues. And I still have a little left, if you would like it back?"

Seeing him laugh, knowing she was the cause of it, knowing they were together: it was too much, too much happiness to bear! And it could all have been lost so easily.

"I am glad I was not a fool for too long," she said quietly. "To think, the ship was but minutes from being too far from the coast to return."

"We both were foolish," he was saying, and her hands were in his and she was not sure who had moved forward or if they had both moved together. "But when . . . when you are in love, it is easy to be so."

Her heart was pounding, stronger and more excited than it had ever been before. Her hands were warm, and her thighs hot, and she wanted to melt into a puddle before him and just adore him.

"Love?" She whispered.

George nodded, and slipped one of his hands over her cheek. "I love you, Florence Capria. I think I will never love anyone as much I love you, and we have a whole lifetime to get to know each other better."

"You are not," Florence said hesitantly. Was she actually going to say this? But she must, she must if she was ever going to know for sure, to be quite sure. "You do not think you will regret this? We have known each other for such a short amount of time, and – "

He did not choose to answer her with words. Instead, his hot and thirsty lips caught up hers and he was kissing her, kissing her like she was water and he was drowning, his hand dropping hers so he could pull her towards him, her softness meeting his hardness as they stood in the centre of his hallway.

They could have been kissing for hours, or just a few seconds. Florence could not tell.

When they broke apart, their hands were entangled in the other's hair, and she saw the desire in his eyes.

"Now then," she said with a warning smile. "You have not made an honest woman of me yet, George. Do not think you can – George, stop!"

But Florence laughed as her future husband swung her into his arms, and started carrying her up the wide sweeping staircase.

"I must insist," George said with a grin. "I absolutely have to show you this old chest Morgan put in my room, 'tis absolutely the best thing for barricading oneself in."

Their mingled laughter echoed in the hallway as they moved towards the top step, where a shocked and confused man was standing, holding an empty glass.

"Would – would sir like another glass of recovery tonic?"

Florence tilted her head, so close as it was to his jawline already she could not help but brush against his cheek, and a shiver of anticipation fluttered through her. Was he actually going to . . ?

"No thank you, Morgan," George said easily. "I think I have all I need to restore me right here."

She could not help but laugh, and her laugh increased as she saw the astonished look on the man's face.

"And who, exactly," the man said pompously as they reached the top step, George pausing to speak to him, "is *this*?"

A raised eyebrow was all that was needed to display his confusion, but Florence did not mind. Nothing could hurt her today, not while she was resting in George's arms.

"This?" George said, an air of mock confusion. "Oh, *this*. This, Morgan, is the future Lady George Northmere."

Without waiting to hear the spluttered reply, George strode just a few more paces and carried her into a room lit by a solitary candle beside the bed.

"You should not have said that," whispered Florence. She did not know exactly why she was whispering, but speaking any louder seemed wrong, somehow.

"Why not?" George whispered back, his breath warming her neck as he lowered his lips onto it. "Within five days, it will be the truth."

Florence wanted to protest, to tell him she would need far more time to organise a wedding than that, and he would want his family to be able to attend, and anyway, he had not actually asked her yet: but all those thoughts melted away as his arms dropped her onto the bed.

"You saved me," George said, his voice unsteady. "When I was lost, you found me."

Florence whetted her lips as she stared up at him, warmth flowing through her body like a sun and parts of her pulsing like the last time they had made love. "I thought I was the one who was lost."

In a swift movement, he was above her, but not overwhelming or heavy. Resting on his arms, he caressed her hair, tangling his fingers in it – and then loosening them so his fingers can dance closer, and closer to her collarbone, and then lower, until she was closing her eyes and arching her back once more in the hope he would eventually reach his goal.

When he grazed past her nipple through her gown, she could not help but cry out quietly.

"We were both lost then," came his husky voice, and he lowered himself gently so she could feel the strength of him, the hardness of his body as it longed for her just as she longed for him. "But neither of us are lost anymore."

"I never want to be again," Florence gasped, her eyelashes fluttering as that same hand moved down her body, and flickered up her skirt to move beneath. "I never want to be without you again."

His crushing kiss stopped her mouth, and she responded eagerly, her hands clutching at him, drawing him closer, bringing him down to her. It was impossible not to moan as his hand reached her hips, lifting her, grasping her, and then caressing her once more, the medley of brusque and soft building in a rhythm that made her legs curl around him, keeping him close.

Florence had no idea how he managed it, but in a swift motion her gown was untied, and he wrenched it from her body like a man possessed.

"I have to have you," he moaned in her ear as his fingers stroked past her breast.

She quivered at his touch and tried to reply, but she had no words, there were no words for this sort of pleasure. Frantic fingers moved to his shirt, but instead of trying each button she wrenched it off, sighing with unadulterated pleasure at the sight of him, at the feel of him as he kissed her once more.

Wave upon wave of sensuality was washing over her now, and Florence could not keep track, his hands and fingers moved so rapidly and so gently and then so strong on her body she thought she could not bear any more – and of course, she must.

She was naked, and so was he, and they were entangled in the bedding and she barely knew where she ended and Lord George Northmere began, and what did it matter because they were of one soul anyway.

"I love you," she gasped, "please – please, George, this pressure, I cannot stand it – "

George shuddered as he dropped his mouth to her breast and she cried out, and she did not care who heard her because this was torture, sweet torture, and it had to end and it could never end –

He entered her slowly and every inch of him sparked more jolts of desire across her body, and her hands found his buttocks and he cried out her name at the touch.

"Oh, Florence," he breathed, "Florence – Florence I am going to give you such ecstasy – "

But he could not finish his sentence because she had already captured his mouth with her own, and he was moving now, moving to their own heartbeats which were one and the same now.

Stars were exploding in Florence's vision as she felt the heady pleasure building and building, and the crest of the wave was coming now and she grabbed hold of his shoulders as if she were to be swept out to sea, just as when they had first met.

They climaxed together, thrashing softly in the linen sheets as the glow settled on them, sweating from their exploits and dazed in their joy.

"I could do that," Florence breathed into his neck as they twisted, and lay beside each other, "every day of our lives."

George chuckled deeply. "Careful, or I will hold you to that."

She smiled gently, ripples of carnal pleasure still washing over her body. "Please do."

12

"Are you completely sure about this?"

George grinned as his brother handed over his silk cravat. "Luke, you worry too much."

Luke scowled, and strode over to the drinks cabinet to pour himself another whisky. "What was it, a week ago you first met this girl?"

There was nothing that he could say to dull George's spirits. "What, you are worried she is out to get my money?" He grinned. "You know I barely have any, and so does she. Please, Luke. Be happy for me."

The two brothers were in the library – George's favourite room in his home – and when the clock over the mantlepiece chimed quarter to the hour, they both glanced over to it.

"Just fifteen minutes to go," said Luke darkly. "Fifteen minutes before you begin your journey to tie yourself to this woman, losing all freedom and – "

"I lose far more without her than with her," George interjected. He was staring into the mirror on the way, attempting to get his cravat straight and completely failing to succeed. "Would you give me a hand with this?"

Luke rolled his eyes, threw his whisky bad-temperedly down onto the table, and returned to the other side of the room. "I just never thought I would be attending your wedding," he said, pulling one side of the cravat so it came completely undone, and starting again. "Seven days. Seven days ago you met Miss Capria, 'tis madness!"

George could not help but smile. He had been true to his word: just five days had passed since they had found each other again, and the church was booked, the flowers arranged, the ring procured, and at eleven o'clock that morning, they would be man and wife.

His brother nodded curtly at the newly arranged cravat, and shook his head with a wry smile. "I suppose nothing but someone incredible would have tempted you to the altar in the first place."

George shook his head. "I could not walk away from her, even if I wanted to. Florence is – she is everything I would want in a woman, and more. Witty, beautiful, caring, insightful – "

"And Italian," Luke interrupted, throwing himself into an armchair. "You may end up living in Rome, or Venice."

The bridegroom laughed. "I suppose I might! There does not seem to be anything I would not do for her, Luke. Losing her would mean losing everything, and if she asked me for anything – but then, she never would."

Luke scoffed. "George, she is too good to be true: mark my words, you will discover something wrong with her!"

George shrugged, and pulled on his top hat. "Perhaps. But then, I am no perfect gentleman either. I think we will be happy."

His brother sighed, rose from the armchair, and picked up his own top hat. "I have never seen you like this, George. I cannot think of anyone more deserving to find their perfect match, and I hope you are right."

"You wait until you meet her," George's eyes shone. "Then you will see."

It was a chilly day that they stepped into as the front door slammed behind them, and George regretted for a moment not throwing a greatcoat over his wedding outfit: but then, what was the point? The church was only two streets away, and before long he would be warmed by the sight of Miss Florence Capria.

"You know, as your best man," Luke said as they strode along the pavement, carefully dodging a young pickpocket who squealed as his fingers were caught moving towards the gentleman's pocketbook, "'tis my duty – and as it aligns with my own curiosity, I will definitely ask it – to enquire whether you did ever find Miss Teresa Metcalfe?"

George grinned at him as they turned the corner. "Worried she will no longer give you a cut of your recommendations?"

His brother's eyebrows rose. "You have a very low opinion of me, dear brother."

"When it is merited, I am afraid I form very firm opinions," shot back George. "No, I did not meet Miss Teresa Metcalfe – and I must say, I have no wish to."

"I wonder what happened to her," Luke said musingly. "Perhaps she met another man, and received a better offer."

"Perhaps she fell into the Thames, or was stolen by pirates," George said with a laugh. "Come on."

The church stood before them, and George started walking up the steps – only to discover that he was doing so alone.

He turned around. "Luke?"

His brother was standing at the bottom step, staring up at him. "We are really going in?"

George stared at him, puzzled. "Well, of course we are. 'Tis a little difficult to wed one's intended from the steps of a church!"

Luke's jaw fell open. "All this time, I think I genuinely thought there was a chance this was all a jest!"

Their shared laughter rang out in the street as a carriage pulled up outside the church.

"God's teeth, we are about to get overtaken by the bride!" Luke said hastily as he ran up the steps. "Quickly, quickly!"

The two brothers burst into the church to receive a very disapproving look from their father; but George completely ignored it due to the sight of two men, seated either side of her, but awkward and embarrassed looks on their faces.

"T-Tom?" George said, coming to an abrupt halt halfway up the aisle. Luke raced past him as he said, "Harry?"

The two gentlemen nodded, but George had no time to further converse with his estranged brothers. The door behind him had opened, and the bride was about to enter the church.

"Hurry, George!" Luke hissed from the altar, and George almost tripped over his own feet in his haste to join his best man.

The door opened, and a solitary figure entered the church.

~

      lorence could feel her heart fluttering in her chest, but it slowed to a calm pace at the sight of Lord George Northmere, standing at the altar beside a man who must be his brother, Luke.

The church was almost empty, but then she had not expected it to be full. She had no family, no friends in this country; George had wanted a small wedding, and she was happy to oblige.

Anything, anything for this man who made her whole being sing out with joy.

The organ began, and completely alone, she started her slow procession up the aisle.

Her fingers tightened around the bouquet of flowers she had made that morning: rosemary and roses, the flowers of true love. Her eyes flickered to the right to see an elegant older woman with two men either side of her – two men who looked awfully familiar, as though she had seen them before through a dark glass, or a rainstorm.

The music changed, and she looked up to lock eyes with George himself. He had turned, he had twisted around to see her, and there was such pride on his face, such happiness it almost brought a tear to her eye.

To think she could bring a man such happiness.

The aisle had seemed long when she had entered the church, but Florence arrived at the altar in what felt like no time at all. George reached out his hand, and she took it. Her hand tingled where he touched it.

"You are the most radiant creature on Earth," he whispered with a smile.

Florence smiled back. "And you are not too shabby either, *Lord* George."

He rolled his eyes as the vicar began the wedding service.

"Dearly beloved, we are gathered here today . . ."

"I could hardly believe it when I came in," George said in an undertone while the vicar droned on, "but my brothers are here."

Florence's eyes widened. "All of them?"

George nodded.

She could not help but grin at his words. She had hoped, she had hoped beyond hope but without knowing the exact details of their estrangement . . .

"I wrote to them," she whispered, glancing over to him. "And very expensive it was too, getting the letters there within a day. I asked them to come; I told them they had already lost so much time, and that they should lose no more. What better moment to reconcile than a wedding?"

The vicar interrupted with, "Do you, Lord George Albert Gerald Northmere, take this woman . . ."

The vows were over before they were begun, and the vicar began the ending speech before he could declare them man and wife.

George's eyes were still wide at her words. "You – you wrote to them?" His grip on her hand tightened. "We are not even married and I already do not deserve you," he said, his smile deepening as he turned to look at his brothers. "Miss Capria, is there nothing you cannot do?"

Florence nodded with a smile. "Just one thing. I am about to lose my name forever and take a new one – and that is something I cannot stop, and have no wish to!"

". . . man and wife!"

"Ah, but when you lose it to a Lord, you know that it is true love," whispered George as he pulled his new wife into a tight embrace and a loving kiss.

Wondering what happened to Teresa? Discover her Ravishing Regencies story in Drenched with a Duke *– read on for the first chapter...*
Please do leave a review if you have enjoyed this book – I love reading your thoughts, comments, and even critiques!
You can also receive my news, special offers, and updates by signing up to my mailing list at www.subscribepage.com/emilymurdoch

DRENCHED WITH A DUKE

CHAPTER ONE

Alexander was not angry. He was fuming.

"And what right does she have," he spat out while striding down the street, his companion struggling to keep up. "Little slip of muslin, I know her brother and he is only just a decent sort of man."

"Slow down," panted Luke. "I am the Marquis of Dewsbury, not a horse – Caershire!"

Alexander found his arm had been grabbed, and swung round to stare at his friend. "What?"

He could not help himself. Rage burned through his lungs, and he wanted to shout and complain until it was all blown out of his body. His dark hair had dropped over his eyes, and his broad shoulders were heaving, heart pounding, feet desperate to keep moving.

"You will do yourself an injury." Luke took in deep breaths, and leaned against the wall they were standing beside. "I swear, Caershire, you will take a step in front of a carriage or pick a fight, I know you of old!"

Alexander grinned. "Perhaps too long, I would say. God's teeth, but you are right."

The tension in his shoulders was starting to dissipate, and the cool of the night air was drying the sweat on his brow.

Luke pulled his cravat, which had become dislodged from its correct position in the rush to leave Almacks, back to its rightful place. "London is no place to wander in anger, Caershire, you should know that by now."

The Duke of Caershire shrugged, but his heart was still beating fast and the injustice of the last hour still rang in his mind. "Miss Josephine Layland had no right to speak to me that way."

Luke's laugh echoed in the deserted street. "Caershire, any woman has the right to reject a man's hand for a dance – where would we be if we could force the beautiful ones to remain on our arms all evening?"

But his friend's laughter did nothing to sooth Alexander's spirits. It had been humiliating: there was no better word for it. There he had been, dressed in all his finery, waiting for her for nigh on two hours, refusing to ask a single other young lady to dance – at great personal cost, for there had been some favours promised to irate mothers which would now have to be explained away – and when Miss Layland had entered the room –

"Already engaged to dance!" He spat, his thoughts finding room in his tongue as he started to walk once more. "A completely full card, that is what she said, and yet I had engaged her for the *La Boulangere* dance what – three days, ago?"

Luke, striding beside his friend, brought out a pocket watch and examined in. "I think you will find it is four days ago, now."

Alexander's eyebrows rose. "Goodness, past midnight already? Oh, Dewsbury, I do not mean to be such bad company. When I get disgruntled – "

"You stay disgruntled," finished Luke, a lazy grin on his face as they passed a gentleman walking in the opposite direction. "Do you not think you should start to mend that habit, now you approach thirty?"

"When you perfect all your character flaws, then you come to me," shot back Alexander, but it was not said in anger. That had drained out of him now, the heat of the moment dissipated as quickly as the anger had risen. All that was left now was bitterness. "Thank you for walking with me, I had no wish to stew in a carriage. Did you hear what she said to me?"

They turned a corner, taking the road that would lead them back to Luke's lodgings.

"No, what did she – "

"She said that she could never deign to accept the hand, for a dance or in matrimony, of a man with such a sullied reputation," said Alexander. He tried to laugh, but it sounded empty even to his own ears. "I mean, can you believe it?"

His companion did not speak, but focused determinedly on the road ahead of them.

Alexander nudged his friend's shoulder. "Well?"

Luke sighed. "Well, what? You think that a Dukedom means that any pretty woman should throw herself at your feet?"

"No, but – "

"You think that you are the only charming man that walks into Almacks?"

Alexander felt a little uncomfortable now. "'Tis not like you to preach, Luke."

Their footsteps had taken them directly to the Marquis of Dewsbury's London apartment, and he sighed when he looked at his friend. "Caershire, you know that I am your friend, and I do not say these words to hurt you – or to embarrass you."

Alexander sighed, and put a hand on his friend's shoulder. "And a better friend, I have not in the world."

Luke grinned. "Careful, or Anthony will be after my blood. No, let me be serious for a moment. The rumours of your reputation notwithstanding – "

"Or lack thereof," interrupted Alexander.

"Are you going to let me speak?"

"Sorry."

Luke smiled ruefully at the tall man opposite him. "I am going back to the family home tomorrow, and yes, that means you will be here in London on your own. I know that this hurts you more than you let on. Just . . . just know that you knew this would happen when you made that decision four years ago. You knew the consequences then. You have to live with them now."

Alexander stared into the dark brown colour eyes of his best friend, and dropped his gaze. "I cannot deny it; and yet I wish that it were not so. If I had known, then . . ."

"You would have made the same decision." Luke grinned, and jerked his head to the door. "I better go in, I am meeting with my brothers tomorrow and I will need all my strength for it."

Alexander returned the smile. He had known the Northmere brothers his entire life, and Luke, as the eldest, rarely missed getting his own way with the family – even if it meant going against his intimidating father.

"Send my best wishes to the Duke," he said.

Luke nodded. "My father, I am sure, sends his regards back."

The two men embraced, and Alexander tried to convey some of the gratitude that he felt to his friend for the last two weeks of companionship. It was difficult; he was not a man who shared his emotions easily, and Luke's constant devil-may-care attitude belied what he truly felt. But if ever a man was a brother to him, it was the Marquis of Dewsbury.

They broke apart.

"Safe journey," said Alexander with a smile.

Luke nodded, and entered his home leaving Alexander alone in the street.

He sighed, and watched his breathe plume before him. His own lodgings were just a few streets away, but his feet itched. This bitterness, this frustration at being – once again – rejected by a beautiful woman, it had to be got rid of before he turned in for the night.

The streets of London were well known to him, and so he made his way to the banks of the Thames. Long and winding, the pathway along the north bank were almost as populated at this midnight hour than during the day.

Hawkers and sellers, a few pedlars and a woman selling hot pies that smelt delicious; Alexander glanced at them all with little care as he strode along by the water's edge.

Somehow, water had always calmed him. He had been like that since a boy, when he and Richard –

The pain shot back into his heart, and Alexander physically shook his head. No need to delve into that again. He had experienced enough heart wrenching today without revisiting his brother's past.

The gas lamps had been sparsely lit down the pathway, so Alexander moved from light to shadow as he paced. Why should he care so much, why should it matter? The memory of the entire room in Almacks quietening as Miss Layland strode away from him, a friend at her side for support. The way that eyes had followed him, greedy in their hunger for gossip, intrigue, and rumour.

The darkening of her eyes as she had beheld him, and rejected him publicly and without honour.

There was physical pain now; Alexander glanced down at his hands, and saw that he had clenched them, digging his nails into his palms until his left hand had started to bleed.

It was intolerable, this stain on his reputation. If things did not change soon, then something drastic had to happen. Perhaps even –

The night was torn apart by a loud scream, and a terrible splash.

As Teresa hit the water, the freezing cold seemed to burn her skin, dragging her down as her skirts became drenched.

An attempt to scream was stifled by the rush of water that flowed into her throat, and her desperate arms moved wildly in an attempt to keep herself afloat.

"Help me!" she spluttered, desperation preventing her mind from knowing that there was no one who could help her.

This could not be happening – she was not going to drown here, she was not going to die! But there seemed little chance of any other outcome as the freezing current started to pull her downwards, and there was nothing she could do, she could not swim, and her head sank under the waves and her hands were the only things still above the water, and this was it, this was how her life ended –

A hand. A strong hand, a hand on hers. Teresa felt it dimly, as though it was happening a thousand miles away from her, but it was definitely a hand, and there was a pain in her shoulder and she could not understand why, and her lungs were on fire and yet her mouth was full of water, and suddenly a rush of water was cascading down her as she was hauled out of the water and dropped onto something that felt as heavenly as earth ...

Teresa took in the deepest breath of her life. Coughing and spluttering, the cold night air absolutely glacial on her skin as it hit the droplets of Thames still dripping from her, her gown sodden and ruined, the silk completely destroyed, she opened her eyes.

Before her were a large pair of men's boots. There were legs inside them.

"What in God's name were you doing in there?"

The words were harsh, from a deep male voice, and cutting in their tone.

Teresa tried to speak, but spluttering was all that she could manage. Her lungs were painful, throbbing pulsated in her throat as she tried again, but her body could do nothing.

"Fool," muttered the same voice, and suddenly a heavy coat was covering her sprawled body.

Heat now rose within her, but it was of shame and embarrassment, not thanks to the greatcoat that enveloped her. To think that she should be seen like this, bedraggled, hair a mess, gown ruined, and by a man of some repute too, if the quality of his greatcoat was anything to go by.

Teresa took another deep breath, and tried once more to speak. "Th-thank you."

It was not enough, she knew, to say to the man who had saved her life, but it was all that she could manage at the moment.

"How did you fall in?" asked the voice, and Teresa pushed herself into a sitting position on the damp ground to look at the face of her rescuer.

He was tall. Seated as she was, Teresa had to tilt her neck backwards to reach his face, and it was only then that she realised that he was just as drenched as she was. He had a dark, olive complexion, dark hair – although perhaps it looked darker because it was wet – and a questioning eye that did not blanch as she examined him.

"I did not fall in," she said eventually, arching an eyebrow with a smile. "I was pushed."

"Pushed?" The man seemed astonished, and despite the cold, wet, and slightly uncomfortable position that she was in, Teresa could not help but smile. It was always reassuring to see that she had what it took to confuse a man.

Teresa nodded, and struggled to her feet. "'Tis of no matter, I assure you."

"No – no matter?" Now it was her rescuer's turn to splutter. "My dear lady, if a man has made an attempt on your life, you should inform the Bow Street Runners, immediately! I will be glad to assist –"

"No," said Teresa curtly. The last thing that she needed was for a peeler to get anywhere near her. At the raised eyebrow of her rescuer, she added, "I am sure it was an accident, and I would be loath to get a gentleman in trouble for an accident."

Now that she was standing, the man's height seemed diminished slightly. The broadness of his shoulders, perhaps, distorted the view, for he was still just as tall, but strong, young like she was, perhaps even a little younger.

Teresa pulled a blonde strand of hair away from her cheek, and smiled. "Now, I have an appointment to make. Do excuse me, sir."

Looking about her, she saw that she was back on the north bank; most inconvenient, as it was going to be a long walk back to the dockyard. Perhaps she could find –

"Appointment?" The man stared at her. "What sort of appointment – with whom?"

Teresa smiled, and removed the greatcoat from her shoulders. "No one of your acquaintance, I am sure, Mr . . ?"

For a moment, she thought she saw a flash of confusion over his face, but then he sighed and said, "Alexander."

"Well, thank you, Mr Alexander, for your kind rescue." Teresa put all her beauty, drenched as it was, into the smile that she gave him. "I certainly do not know what I would have done if you had not come along, but I am quite safe now."

She reached out the greatcoat, but he did not take it. "It is not Mr Alexander, actually. 'Tis just, Alexander. That is my name."

Why did he not take the coat? Teresa tried to keep her smile on her face, but it was a little more brittle now. She was late to meet Lord George Northmere as it was, and if she missed it, she was unlikely to get a second chance.

"Alexander? Surely you have a surname?"

He looked even more uncomfortable at this, and Teresa could not sense why. There was such a simplicity about him, really, completely unlike most of the men she knew.

But she did not have time to play naming games with a stranger on the bank of the Thames. She had somewhere to be.

Throwing the greatcoat over one of his shoulders, Teresa said gaily, "Well, whoever you are, thank you. Good evening."

She turned away from him, and began to walk briskly – partly to reach Lord George in time, and partly, in truth, to keep warm.

Hurried footsteps followed her, and she rolled her eyes before Alexander reached her side.

"But you cannot just – you are soaking wet!"

"Yes, I am aware of that, thank you," Teresa attempted to keep the sarcasm out of her voice, but it was incredibly difficult with such a silly man. Why could he not leave her alone? "And yet I am almost sure I know the remedy for that, so good evening to you."

He was a handsome man, she could see that now. That olive complexion, that chiselled and finely shaved jaw, that essence of strength that a man either had or had not. You could not replicate it, you could not pretend.

This Alexander had it in spades.

"My dear lady – what is your name?"

Teresa was attempting to increase her pace, but the dratted man was just as quick as she was. "Teresa."

They rounded a bend in the river, and passed a gaggle of revellers, undoubtedly thrown out by one of the gentleman's clubs. Teresa swore under her breath. If she did not find Lord George soon, she would be too late to take advantage of throwing out time, and then she would be in a difficult spot.

"Teresa . . . you must have a surname."

Alexander placed a hand on her arm as he attempted to slow her down. "Surely you cannot be any sort of real rush, Miss – "

"I am," she said, wrenching her arm away from him and glaring at him. "Miss Metcalfe, not that it means a thing to you, Mr . . ?"

If she had not known better, she would have said that he looked a little embarrassed.

"Duke, actually."

She did not have time for this, every second wasted on this man was one that she was losing with Lord George. "As I said, thank you, Mr Duke, for helping me out of the river, but there really is no need to accompany me."

And yet he still did not disappear, even when she started walking again. "I am not Mr Duke, I am a Duke."

That was enough to stop her in her tracks. Teresa flew around to stare at him. "A Duke?"

Alexander grinned at her, almost apologetically. "Duke of Caershire, believe it or not."

Teresa stared at him, calculating. Well, knowing that he was a Duke certainly turned things around a bit; now that she took a closer look, she could see the unmistakable signs of wealth. But pennies in your pocket were worth more than guineas in someone else's, and she had no time to waste.

"I would have curtseyed, had I known," she said with a cheeky grin, and she saw the answering preen in his stance that she knew would come. My, but weren't men predictable? "Good evening, my lord."

His surprised face drew level with hers, even though she was walking as fast as she could – almost running. "You – you do not want my protection?"

"I do not need your protection," Teresa said hurriedly, and with just a little of her irritation seeping through. "To tell the truth, my lord, I have somewhere to be, and it is not a somewhere that you should be seen. Go away."

Darting down a side alley, Teresa broke out into a run – anything to be rid of this puppy of a Duke. But she had underestimated him; his reflexes were quick, and so were his feet, and within twenty seconds he had caught up with her, caught hold of her, and thrust her against a wall.

"God's teeth, let go of me!" Teresa cried, and then, in a desperate hope that the knowledge would release her, exclaimed, "I am a courtesan, you fool!"

HISTORICAL NOTE

I always strive for accuracy with my historical books, as a historian myself, and I have done my best to make my research pertinent and accurate. Any mistakes that have slipped in must be forgiven, as I am but a lover of this era, not an expert.

ABOUT THE AUTHOR

Emily Murdoch is a historian and writer. Throughout her career so far she has examined a codex and transcribed medieval sermons at the Bodleian Library in Oxford, designed part of an exhibition for the Yorkshire Museum, worked as a researcher for a BBC documentary presented by Ian Hislop, and worked at Polesden Lacey with the National Trust. She has a degree in History and English, and a Masters in Medieval Studies, both from the University of York. Emily has a medieval series, a Regency series, and a Western series published, and is currently working on several new projects.

You can follow her on twitter and instagram @emilyekmurdoch, find her on facebook at www.facebook.com/theemilyekmurdoch, and read her blog at www.emilyekmurdoch.com

11139441R00064

Printed in Germany
by Amazon Distribution
GmbH, Leipzig